HYPERSPACE HIGH

THE SCHOOL THAT'S OUT OF THIS WORLD

HYPERSPACE HIGH

GALACTIC BATTLE

ZAC HARRISON

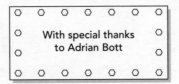

With special thanks
to Adrian Bott

First published in 2013 by Curious Fox,
an imprint of Capstone Global Library Limited,
7 Pilgrim Street, London, EC4V 6LB
Registered company number: 6695582

www.curious-fox.com

Text © Hothouse Fiction Ltd 2013

Series created by Hothouse Fiction
www.hothousefiction.com

The author's moral rights are hereby asserted.

Cover Illustration by Dani Geremia

ISBN 978 1 78202 004 2

1 3 5 7 9 10 8 6 4 2

A CIP catalogue for this book is available from the British Library.

Typeset in Avenir by Hothouse Fiction Ltd

Printed and bound by CPI Group (UK) Ltd, Croydon, CR0 4YY

MIX
Paper from
responsible sources
FSC® C020471

For Henry and Beatrice

CHAPTER 1

John Riley's shared dorm was like a plush hotel room, with luxurious sofas and vast enclosed beds. And the floor-to-ceiling window had a view that no hotel on Earth could have matched. But as John gazed out at black outer space twinkling with stars, he couldn't help wishing instead for a view of trees and grass. He longed to see a clear blue sky with fluffy white clouds. It had been several weeks since he'd left Earth, and he was feeling a bit homesick for his world. John let out a deep sigh.

"What's wrong, John?" his room-mate Kaal asked.

"Oh, nothing," John replied, forcing a smile. "Just

missing home a bit."

"I know exactly how you feel," Kaal said sympathetically. "I can't wait to see my folks at the Space Specta—" Kaal cut himself off abruptly, before continuing awkwardly. "Sorry, John. I keep forgetting that your parents can't come."

A gloomy silence descended over their room. But it was soon broken by the sound of an incoming video call. Suddenly, three demonic, green-skinned figures filled one of the two video screens on the desk. They leaned in close, their wings rustling behind them, and grinned, revealing white, shark-like teeth.

Kaal, who looked exactly like the aliens on the screen, grinned back at them and waved happily. "Hi, Mum! Hi, Dad! It's so good to see you! How's little Varka? Hi, Kulvi. Hey, you've had your teeth sharpened! Nice!"

"You're looking well, son," rumbled the largest alien, who John guessed was Kaal's father. "Varka is sleeping, thank goodness. She's finally had her first skin-shedding— Ah, I didn't realize your room-mate was there, too! Hello, John."

John, who was sprawled on one of the sofas, looked

up from his holocomic. "Wide skies, Mr Tartaru," he said, giving the traditional Derrilian greeting Kaal had taught him. Even though Kaal and his family were speaking their native language, John could understand every word they were saying, thanks to Hyperspace High's computer system, which translated everything into the language of each individual listener.

"And good flight to you, too, young man!" Kaal's father responded, clearly impressed.

"What excellent manners your friend has," said Kaal's mother.

"Wonder where he learned them?" Kulvi said, with warmth and wickedness in her voice. "Surely not from my little brother Kaal. You want to watch out for him, John; he's a savage. Hey, Kaal. Remember when you put the scutterliches in my bed?"

"They needed somewhere warm to hatch or they'd have died!" Kaal protested.

John tried not to laugh. He'd heard Kaal's side of this story a hundred times.

"Now, Kaal," his mother said, "this chit-chat is very pleasant, but we must discuss our visit to Hyperspace High. There are only three days to go."

"I know," Kaal said, fidgeting with excitement. "I can't wait!"

"We're looking forward to it too, dear one. But there are arrangements to make! Did you reserve a docking space for the family starhopper? We won't be the only family coming to visit! And where are we going to sit during the Space Spectacular? You can't leave these things to the last minute, you know."

John grinned and retreated behind his holocomic, leaving Kaal to chat excitedly to his family.

It was funny how mums and dads were much the same all over the galaxy, if Kaal's were anything to go by. His own mother would have been just as fussy about the arrangements. John idly wondered what his mum and dad would make of Kaal's family. They'd probably run screaming ... like John nearly had, the first day he'd met Kaal.

"Hey, do you know if the Tarz family is coming?" Kulvi said. "I haven't seen Brannicus Tarz in years! He's a bigwig on the Galactic Council now."

"Of course they are!" Kaal said. "This *is* the Space Spectacular we're talking about. Everyone's family is coming!" Then he stopped in his tracks. "Um. Almost everyone's, I mean. Not all the families can make it, of course."

"Of course," his father echoed. There was another awkward silence.

John winced. Neither Kaal nor his family had looked in John's direction, but he knew they were talking about him. He was the only student on Hyperspace High whose parents would never – *could* never – visit the school.

It wasn't just the distance. Unlike all the other parents, John's mum and dad didn't even know he was here on Hyperspace High. They thought he was at a boarding school back on Earth. All those weeks ago, John had accidentally climbed aboard a space shuttle that he'd thought was the coach taking him to his new boarding school in Derbyshire. Instead, he was taken far away into the galaxy, to the best space school in the universe: Hyperspace High. John, the first Earthling to ever board the school, had almost been expelled seconds after arriving – here, that meant being thrown out of an airlock! It was only thanks to the intervention of Lorem, the school's headmaster, that John had been allowed to stay on as a pupil.

So far, John had managed to keep his parents thinking that he was at the Earth boarding school. There had been a few narrow escapes, though, like the time he'd had to pretend an alien in his room was a science project. That had been a close shave ...

"Do you two even know what you're doing for the Spectacular?" Kulvi asked.

"We haven't even been assigned to our groups yet," Kaal said. "That's happening at twelve sharp today, in the Centre. I might get Galactic Battle, Plasma Sculpting, Zero-G Acrobatics – even Star Dance! Can you imagine me dancing?"

"I was a Star Dancer in my final year, remember?" Kulvi said, laughing. "I'll never forget it. We were like a herd of gograflomps in rehearsal! Nearly demolished the stage!"

"Great," Kaal said. "That's an encouraging thought."

"Hey, if we could pull it off, you can. It all came together in the end, thank goodness. We rocked that Spectacular."

"I'm sure Kaal will make us proud, whatever activity he's assigned to," Kaal's dad said.

"I'll do my best, Father," Kaal said gravely, as if his life depended on it.

John rolled his eyes behind his comic. His huge Derrilian friend was fun to be around, but he could be very serious sometimes, especially where his family was concerned. Although John knew he'd be just as keen to impress his own parents if they were coming.

John idly wondered what activity he'd be assigned to. Honestly, he wasn't even sure what a Space Spectacular was. A sort of cross between an open day and a school show, he guessed, where all the students showed off the skills they'd learned, while the families looked on. By the sound of it, it was a pretty big deal. Families would soon be arriving at Hyperspace High from worlds many light years away.

Not from Earth, though.

John sighed, put down the comic, and squeezed his eyes shut to stop himself from crying. It was hard to pretend that everything was OK while listening to Kaal and his family make plans.

Kaal was still talking excitedly. "... and when the Spectacular's finished, can we go out for a meal at

Ska's Café? They do the best Vortex lumpgriddles *anywhere ...*"

John thought back to the last time he'd taken part in a show in front of parents. He'd been the lead in the school production of *Oliver*, and he'd sung his heart out. His mum had been so happy, she'd cried. "I'd do anyfing for youuuu," he'd sung to her in the car on the way home, over and over, until she was laughing.

What was that cold, empty, sucking feeling behind his ribs, like a black hole draining away his good mood? Oh, yeah. Homesickness. Just being away from home was one thing, but being millions and millions of kilometres away was something else.

Why wasn't there some way for his parents to come, too? It wasn't fair. This enormous space-faring school could travel faster than light, but even if the ship made a detour to visit Earth, he still couldn't bring them on board. Humans hadn't yet made official contact with other galactic beings yet, and that was how it had to stay for now. Rules were rules, and John was very lucky to be the exception.

The dorm door opened, and in bounced Emmie

Tarz, John's golden-skinned, pointy-eared Sillaran friend. "Morning, boys! Have I got some news for— Oh, *hi*, Mr and Mrs Tartaru! Hi, Kulvi! Sorry, I didn't know Kaal was on the vidphone!"

"Hi, Emmie," John said, trying to sound happier than he felt.

Emmie wasn't fooled for a second. In a series of graceful leaps, she crossed the room to the sofa where John lay, her silver hair trailing behind her. "Just the human being I wanted to see. Come on, mister. You're going for a ride."

Before John could protest, she had grabbed his arm and pulled him out of the dorm. "See you later, Kaal! Bye, everyone!"

"What's this about a ride?" John blustered, as Emmie led him down the corridor.

"Thought it might cheer you up," Emmie said, grinning.

"I didn't say anything about being miserable!"

"No. You didn't have to, did you?"

John had to smile. Some things he just couldn't hide, not from Emmie. "So what are we riding?"

"Ah! Well, Sergeant Jegger asked me if I wanted to

do a special assignment for extra credit."

"You agreed to do *extra* schoolwork?" John was surprised by this, as Emmie struggled with most academic subjects.

"I know, right? But this is Space Flight we're talking about. The best class of all, by light years."

"So what's the assignment?"

Emmie grabbed John's shoulders, her blue eyes huge, and spoke slowly. "He wants me to ... wait for it ... test drive a new model t-dart!"

"Wow!" said John. The current t-darts were already awesome. He couldn't imagine what a new one would be like!

"Jegger's thinking of upgrading all the school's t-darts to the new models," Emmie went on. "But he wants to make sure they're still OK to learn in. So he's asked me to take one out for a spin and see what I think."

"Because you're one of the best pilots this school's got," John said.

"Oh, hush," Emmie said, though she was smiling. "I just love flying, that's all. Here we are. Hangar eighty-seven. Feast your eyes on this!"

16

The brand new training dart stood in the hangar, bathed in a single spotlight. Like the older models, it was a sleek, sharp-nosed ship with short, swept-back wings at the rear and a transparent bubble cockpit. But every centimetre of its metallic surface gleamed like silver – even the chrome-like rims of the blast turbines were sparkling clean, not sooty from exhaust fumes like every other t-dart he'd seen.

Emmie pressed her keycard to the side of the craft and the bubble cockpit silently slid open. Inside were two seats, plush and billowy, and each with an identical set of controls.

"Should we suit up?" John asked.

"The manual says we don't need to," Emmie said. "Helmets only. I wonder what that's about?"

"Nice seats!" John said, stroking the soft fabric. A tiny light came on in the console as he did so, and a voice purred, "Human and Sillaran life forms detected. Adjusting settings for maximum comfort."

"Wow," breathed Emmie. "Train in this ship? I could *live* in it!"

"Check this out!" John said, settling himself in his seat as the bubble closed above them. "Onboard drinks dispenser, snack bar, holovid player ... Talk about luxury options!"

As their safety harnesses automatically fastened around them, John and Emmie pulled on their helmets. Instantly the ship's soft voice whispered, "Activating SecondSkin spacesuit nano-weave."

A tickling sensation spread over John's body. He looked down and, to his amazement, saw a silvery layer of fabric spreading out over his chest, arms, and legs. He'd worn a SecondSkin before – they clung to you like a second skin, hence the name – but this one was being woven around him as he sat there!

"Nano-weave microbots!" Emmie said, holding up her hand and watching the fabric glide over it like a liquid-metal glove. "Microscopic machines that can create a spacesuit around you. Now that's tailoring!"

"You'll never have to worry about forgetting your spacesuit again!" John laughed.

"OK," said Emmie, sounding businesslike now that the suits were complete. "Let's see how she handles in flight. Ready to go?"

"Are you kidding? Fire her up!"

Emmie ran a pre flight check, powered up the main

turbine, and ignited the engines. John's stomach was a tight knot of excitement as the take-off sequence counted down and the hangar doors slid open space.

The view always took John's breath away, no matter how many times he saw it – diamond-bright stars shining in the infinite darkness of space. It was amazing enough to see space through the ship's countless windows, but flying out among those stars in a tiny craft like this was just incredible. It made him feel very small, and full of wonder.

"Easy does it," Emmie muttered, carefully steering the little ship up and out of the hangar. "When we're a safe distance away from Hyperspace High, I'll open her up a bit. See what she can do."

That was Emmie all over, John thought. She loved the thrills, but she'd never put anyone at risk. No wonder she was the favourite student of Sergeant Jegger, the three-legged Space Flight instructor.

"OK. This is a *smooth* ship," Emmie said, banking them around so that they were flying alongside Hyperspace High. "The intertial compensation works like a dream."

"What the heck's that?" John laughed. "And since

when did you get technical?"

She stuck out her tongue. "It's a new flight feature. The ship makes tiny corrections so you don't oversteer." She pursed her lips. "Though maybe that's making things *too* easy. People won't learn if the ship does the job for them ..."

John stared through the bubble at Hyperspace High beside them, looking a bit like an enormous cruise liner. Through thousands of windows and transparent panels, he could see students and teachers walking the halls, sitting in classes, or enjoying a snack. Down in the lower levels, huge robots and machines were working hard.

They flew further and further, and still the huge ship lay beside them. *It's amazing how big Hyperspace High really is,* John thought. *I've been here nearly a term now, and I sort of know my way around, but there are so many places I haven't been. Places still to explore ...*

"That's far enough," Emmie said, once they had finally put the ship behind them. "Time to try some fancy stuff. Hold on tight!"

Emmie put the little t-dart through its paces,

throwing it into barrel rolls, swift zigzag turns, and finishing with a starfire flip – spinning the dart back to face the other way and using the main thrusters as a brake. It was like riding the best roller coaster in the universe.

Emmie finally slowed the t-dart back down to a steady cruise. "I think this model gets the Emmie Tarz seal of approval," she said, patting the console affectionately. "Want to take the controls?"

"You bet!" John said.

Emmie switched the input to John's set of controls. She selected an iced Brucko juice from the drinks dispenser and plugged it into her helmet, then lay back in the sumptuous seat watching the stars go by and sipping through the helmet straw.

John fired up the hyperdrive, sending the little t-dart thundering through the gulfs of space. He felt weightless, joyful, and free, with all the promise of deep space open before him. He could skim the surface of a gas giant or watch a supernova engulf the skies. John grinned to himself. *There might be some drawbacks to studying here at Hyperspace High*, he thought, *like not being able to tell Mum and Dad where I really am ... but I wouldn't swap it for the world. At a boarding school on Earth, I would never get to fly through space with a cool girl from a different planet!*

He glanced over at Emmie. Just when he'd been feeling miserable and homesick, she'd turned up and taken his mind right off it. *I'm lucky to have her as a friend*, he thought. *There aren't that many people who can tell when you're bottling sadness up inside you – and then do something about it.*

From their studies of Galactic Geography, John knew there was an abandoned planet nearby that looked a bit like Earth. John flew the t-dart over the ruins of an alien city that glittered in the pale light from the sun, then out over a frozen sea.

"Cool!" Emmie said with a whistle. "We'd better take her home now, though, or we'll be late."

"I just want to get a better look – it reminds me a bit of home," said John, flying closer to the shining world. He steered the t-dart on a quick game of thread-the-needle with a derelict ring-shaped space station, flying the craft dead centre through the hole in the middle without even needing to use the computer assist. Emmie was right – the ship did handle like a dream.

"Let's get going, John," Emmie said, a little nervously. "We don't want to be late."

Another short blast on the hyperdrive brought them back alongside Hyperspace High in no time. John brought the t-dart around in a sweeping arc, past the colossal bridge section at the front of the massive vessel and back towards the hangar. Soon after, they gently touched down inside it.

Emmie pulled off her helmet and shook her hair free. "Phew. We must have been out there for ages!"

"Can't have been more than half an hour, surely?" said John, but he felt a little uneasy. He'd lost all sense of time while flying the t-dart.

As they tried to leave the hangar, the smooth white form of an Examiner moved to block their way. John felt more than uneasy now. There was something faintly sinister about the faceless, hovering robots. They were frighteningly efficient at their job, which was to enforce the school's many rules. Most of the time they would leave you alone, but if you stepped out of line, they had ways of setting you straight.

Emmie gulped. "Is ... everything OK? We were just leaving—"

"NEGATIVE," the Examiner said in a flat electronic voice, glaring at them with its single red digital eye. "STUDENTS RILEY AND TARZ HAVE VIOLATED RULES."

"What did we do?" John asked nervously.

"STUDENTS WERE INSTRUCTED TO BE PRESENT IN THE CENTRE AT TWELVE SHARP. CURRENT TIME: TWELVE ZERO SEVEN."

"Oh no!" Emmie groaned. "This doesn't sound good."

"I'm so sorry I made us late, Emmie," John said, feeling more miserable than ever.

"TEACHER PERMISSION NOT DETECTED. EMERGENCY NOT DETECTED. CONCLUSION: ABSENCE WAS WILFUL."

John braced himself.

"PUNISHMENT WILL BE DETENTION."

CHAPTER 2

"I can't believe that stupid machine wants us to give up our whole lunch hour for detention," John grumbled. "I was looking forward to lunch!"

"We were only seven minutes late!" Emmie agreed. Sighing, she added, "But you can't reason with the Examiners, and you can't argue – they don't want to know!"

John and Emmie reached the entrance to the Centre. "Come on," John urged. "Kaal's bound to have saved us a place ..."

John's voice died away as the doors opened the Centre. For the students, the Centre was the beating heart of Hyperspace High, a place of shops and cafés where they could go to relax, gossip, or just hang out together. It was like the school's own private shopping mall, light years ahead of anything any Earth school could offer. It was beautiful, too, with a sparkling lake in the middle surrounded by deep-green trees. Around the sides of the massive space were many levels of balconies, which housed a great variety of restaurants.

But today it looked completely different. All the windows, which usually gave a view of starry space, were now flat black. Even the huge dome above the Centre was like a convex black mirror.

John stood dumbfounded, trying to take it all in. It was the Centre, but it had been transformed almost beyond recognition. The balconies around the sides had somehow extended, joining up with one another to form viewing galleries like those in a sports arena, and the tables where the students usually ate had disappeared.

Where is Kaal? John thought. He could see students chatting excitedly between themselves, lounging on bloated, rubbery black cushions that looked like bean bags. These MorphsSeats engulfed the students like a strange jelly, adjusting to support all the different alien body types. But there was no sign of John's big Derrilian friend. Trying to find him among all the students would be like looking for a red dwarf in the Milky Way.

It was proving hard to see anything at all in this auditorium. It was all so black – the windows, the cushions, the balconies. The only bright spot in the whole auditorium was where the central lake used to be. It was now a dazzling white stage the size of a football pitch, made from some sort of translucent material and lit from within. It was throbbing, a band of light sweeping from one end to the other and then back again. Two Examiners stood by the stage, as if they were guarding something invisible, or that hadn't yet appeared.

John snapped back to reality, as Emmie was tugging on his arm. "They haven't started yet! Quick, let's sit down before the Examiners give us any more hassle!"

Together, they worked their way along an elongated balcony, squeezing past students sprawled on their cushions, trying to find empty seats. John felt like someone turning up late to the cinema.

Eventually, they found two empty seats on the very far right of the arena, tucked away near an emergency exit. At the exact moment John sank into his seat, Lorem, the headmaster, shimmered into being on the stage. Lorem looked remarkably like an old human being, with a bald head and wrinkle-lined face, and he sometimes reminded John of a monk. But his strange purple eyes were anything but human, and when you saw him turn into a ball of energy, the resemblance vanished completely. The headmaster also had the very non-human talent of being able to see into the future.

Right now, he was a truly striking sight. Lorem always had a faint glow around him, but in the midst of all this blackness and lit from beneath by the stage, he flared with light like an angelic being.

With his palms up, Lorem held up his hands, and the chatter among the students fell silent, as suddenly as if someone had turned down the volume.

"Thank you, everyone," he said, and his voice seemed to carry around the whole room, though John couldn't see a microphone anywhere. "I'd like to say a few words about the Space Spectacular. I'm sure you're all looking forward to it as much as I am."

Lorem put his hands behind his back and strolled to the edge of the stage. "So, what *is* the Space Spectacular? It is a show – the greatest show in the galaxy, I like to believe. Every year, we open the school to our students' families and invite them to watch as the students demonstrate their skills. I want you to understand that this will not just be a handpicked few. Every single student in the school will have an opportunity to shine."

Once again, John felt excluded. His family wouldn't be here, not this year, nor any other. But he still wanted to shine, just like everyone else.

"We demand a lot from our students, and the visiting families always have very high expectations of the show. I don't intend to disappoint any of them."

Lorem paused and looked out over the silent, awed students with his sparkling eyes. "I will announce which teams you have all been assigned to in a moment. First, it is my duty to issue a warning. Although this is a time of high spirits, which I hope you will all enjoy, school rules are still in full effect."

John shifted uncomfortably in his seat. He didn't really want to hear more talk of rules right now, especially not from the headmaster.

But Lorem's voice was very grave. "For those who do not comply, there will be punishment. Any student who accrues two or more detentions will not be allowed to participate in the Space Spectacular."

Another pause, as those words sunk in. *I've already got one detention*, John thought glumly.

"And now for the teams!" Lorem announced brightly, quickly banishing John's dark mood. "Some roles will be big, some small, but all are equally important. Please sit quite still and do not leave your seats. You will soon understand why."

From high above, a rainbow of light beams suddenly flashed out over the arena. Each one bathed a different student in coloured light – red, yellow, purple, green, blue, pink, and blinding white. Delighted gasps rang out.

"The colour of your light indicates your team, as you will no doubt have guessed," said Lorem, sounding amused. "Let me explain what each colour means."

John was sitting in a shaft of golden-yellow

light. Just like everyone else, he'd been chosen for something, as he knew he would be, but somehow he still felt more excited than he'd expected. John tried to see who else was on his team. However, no matter how hard he looked, he couldn't make out any other students under a yellow beam. There were just too many colours shining down, like a forest of tinted lasers.

"I guess we're not on the same team, then," Emmie said from her neighbouring seat. John looked over and saw that she was sitting in the glare of a blue light.

"I guess not," he said, feeling a little disappointed. He hoped he'd know at least one person on his team. Maybe he'd be with Kaal.

"I wonder what I'll be doing," said Emmie. But she didn't have to wait long to find out.

"Those in blue," Lorem announced next, "will be the Zero-G Acrobatics team."

"Wooo! Best. Spectacular. Ever!" Emmie cheered.

John and Emmie traded a high five, as they'd been doing since John taught his friends the Earth custom. The excitement in the auditorium was so intense now that Lorem had to call for silence before he could read out the remainder of the teams.

Those bathed in purple were the Star Dance team, and try as he might, John couldn't find Kaal to see if he was on that team, either. He crossed his fingers, hoping as hard as he could that they'd end up on the same team.

Green was Plasma Sculpting, white was Traditional Music (John wondered which planet's traditions Lorem could possibly mean), pink was Alien Life Form Training, and red was Live Holo-Theatre, which Emmie explained; it sounded like theatre on Earth, only with holographic scenery, special effects, and costumes projected over the actors.

"Last but not least," Lorem said, "those in yellow will be the Galactic Battle team. For safety reasons, this is the smallest team of all and will be demonstrating a variety of energy weapons."

There was a chorus of *oohs* and *aahs*. John could hardly keep himself from jumping up and yelling with delight. Energy weapons – how unbelievably cool was that?

"Congrats!" Emmie whispered, nudging him and

grinning.

"Thanks! I wish you could be on my team – I really do!"

"Ah, it's cool," she smiled. "To be honest, I'm not much of a weapons fan."

"I wish you all a very successful practice period," Lorem said. "Next time we meet together in this auditorium, many of your families will be here. They will be expecting you to give your very best performance. Let's give them a show to remember!"

With that, he transformed into a tiny ball of sparkling light, sped over the students' heads towards the exit, and vanished up the corridor. It was his preferred method for moving quickly about the ship, like a space-age will-o'-the-wisp.

"ALL STUDENTS ARE NOW DISMISSED," intoned the Examiners as one. "LUNCH HOUR WILL NOW COMMENCE."

"No lunch hour for us," John grumbled. "Come on, Emmie. We've got a detention to get to."

"Yeah," said Emmie, winking. "Thanks to you, Earth boy."

But as Emmie tried to make her way back from the

balcony to the main corridor, the black-haired form of Mordant Talliver moved in front of her, blocking her path. Above his shoulder, like an annoying second robotic head, hovered the silvery sphere of G-Vez, Mordant's Serve-U Droid.

Mordant was wearing a big smug smile on his face, and his two black rubbery tentacles were crossed over his chest.

John braced himself for trouble. The half-Gargon boy was the closest thing Hyperspace High had to a class bully, and he was no friend of John's – nor Emmie's. It didn't help that he was top of just about every class right now, and he looked down on John as a primitive life form from a hopeless backward planet. In Mordant's eyes, John was little better than a caveman – not that Mordant really saw any of the other students as his equal, either.

"Hello, Mordant," Emmie said reluctantly. "Can I get past, please?"

"Oh, sure!" Mordant said, smiling even more broadly. He reminded John of the sort of deep-sea fish that swallows its prey in one gulp. "I just wanted to tell you how happy I am to be on your team. It's an honour."

Emmie looked perplexed. "Um ... er ... thanks?"

"Seriously, I can't wait to get started," Mordant said. "You're the best zero-G gymnast I've ever known. And you know I don't like to boast, but I'm pretty good myself. Our team is going to rock this Spectacular, just you wait."

Emmie looked over at John with an open mouth. Her navy-blue eyes were as wide and blank as the screen of a crashed ThinScreen. John felt much the same, but a deep suspicion was forming in his mind.

Mordant sighed, still not letting Emmie through. "I just wish my dad could see how cool our performance is going to be."

"Unfortunately, master's father is unable to attend," G-Vez explained, unprompted. "He has important business to attend to, as the owner of the most successful intergalactic mining company in the universe. Such riches and responsibility will all be in master's hands one day."

"I guess I'll just have to do my best to impress *your* parents instead, won't I, Emmie?" Mordant said, smiling and patting the beautiful Sillaran on the shoulder. Then he stood aside and waved her through, smiling all the while. When they had passed him, Mordant vanished into the crowd.

Out in the corridor, John shook his head. "What on Earth just happened?"

"I have no idea," said Emmie. "Maybe Mordant's turning over a new leaf? I hope so. That would be really nice."

"Maybe he is," John said, but he was far from convinced. He didn't want to say it out loud and bring up unpleasant memories, but Mordant had been viciously cruel to Emmie in the past. She struggled with some of her subjects, and Mordant just loved to rub her face in that fact.

If he was being nice to her face now, John thought, it could only mean one thing: Mordant Talliver had something troublesome planned. Emmie obviously wanted to believe he'd changed, but she could be too nice for her own good. John thought perhaps he should warn her of his suspicions.

"Emmie, I don't really think—"

"John, look!"

Emmie had interrupted to point to an Examiner gliding towards them from the other end of the corridor.

"Come on, we need to go to detention! Quickly!"

John hurried after Emmie, hoping the Examiner hadn't seen them dawdling.

"If we're late for our lunch-time detention, that'll mean even more punishment!" Emmie whispered. "They'll give us another detention, most likely. And two detentions—"

"—means no Space Spectacular for either of us," John finished.

CHAPTER 3

"I'm *so* relieved you're on my team!" Kaal told John. It was the next morning, and they were heading out along the gleaming-white corridors of Hyperspace High to meet the rest of the Galactic Battle team. "I don't know what I'd do if I didn't have someone I knew to talk to."

John imagined his shy Derrilian friend standing with his back to the wall in a room full of students, too tongue-tied to talk to anyone.

"I know, it's awesome that we're together," John agreed. What were the odds that out of hundreds of pupils he and his best friend would be in the same team? He started trying to calculate exactly what the chances had been, but he was distracted by the view of space from the floor-to-ceiling windows along the left side of the corridor. They were so spotlessly clean, you could barely tell there was anything there at all; the corridor seemed like a balcony space itself.

As John stared out into space, an Examiner rounded the corner, gliding steadily along the corridor, its crimson eye tracking left and right. John held his breath and looked nervously at Kaal. But the Examiner passed John without sparing him even a glance. *Phew.* John allowed himself a deep intake of the recycled atmosphere, as yesterday's encounter surfaced yet again in his thoughts.

What happened yesterday was too freaking close. I'm going to have to be extra careful from now on, especially if Mordant's planning something. And I'm sure he is.

John tried to put his worries to the back of his mind and instead focus on the Space Spectacular. "Hey, where are we meant to meet the others?" he asked Kaal as they continued along the corridor.

"Force field 1.0. It's on the modular energy level."

John frowned. "Funny name for a room. Why's it called that?"

"You could call it a high-tech classroom," Kaal explained, "but it's not really a room at all. Sometimes it doesn't even exist."

"Huh? You've lost me!"

"The whole modular energy deck is one big empty space. The teachers make rooms in it with force-field projectors. They can add new rooms or remove them, or merge them together in any arrangement they like."

"Sounds pretty cool," John admitted. *And if the team is going to practise with energy weapons*, he thought to himself, *it'll help that there aren't any real walls to damage!*

But as they walked up a transparent tunnel of force to reach the classroom and entered the space, John realized he hadn't counted on one little fact: that rooms made from force fields had almost invisible walls and floors. Even the furniture inside it was made from shaped force fields. It was a bit disconcerting to look through the walls into other force-field classrooms, where other teams were meeting, or through the floor at the *real* floor far below.

At least the team looked eager to get started. Three beings had looked up excitedly as John and Kaal entered the room.

John recognized one of the students immediately. "Hi, Kritta! Are you ready to rock?"

"Totally," Kritta said, laughing. She was an insect-like first-year, with six spindly looking legs and eyes formed from hundreds of hexagonal facets. Once you got over how strange she looked, though, you saw her eyes were very beautiful, like gleaming precious jewels. John knew better than to judge Kritta by first appearances anyway. The quiet Centravian didn't always have much to say, but John knew that she could be brave when it mattered. She'd proven that on the planet Kerallin when their class had saved the scholars, the founders of Hyperspace High. John still couldn't quite believe that had only happened a couple of weeks earlier!

The student standing next to Kritta looked surprisingly like a human-sized tree frog. He was bright orange, the same day-glo colour as an Earth road worker's safety jacket. "Hi. I'm Tarope," he said, giving John a smile that was almost a metre wide.

"Hey!" said the third student, a pulsing red oblong that hovered in the air. "You're John Riley, right?" Two short hands protruded from each side of her strange body. John couldn't be sure if she was a super-advanced robot, some sort of intelligent talking crystal, or something he hadn't even heard of before.

"Of course he is," Kritta butted in. "Don't you know a Robot Warriors champion when you see one?"

The red oblong bobbed up and down, as if it were annoyed. "Thought so. I'm Monix. This is my final year, so I'm hoping to go out on a high note. Let's not mess this up, OK?"

"Are there really only five of us?" John wondered aloud.

"Hey, there's actually six – don't forget me!" piped a shrill little voice from somewhere below John's knee.

John looked down to see a tiny yellow creature, no more than thirty centimetres high. She looked a bit like a yellow seahorse, but with delicate little arms and legs. Her beady little eyes were as bright as polished coins.

"Oh, heck," John said, feeling bad. "I'm so sorry, I

didn't see you down there!"

The tiny student laughed, making a sound like a piccolo flute. "Oh, don't worry. I get that all the time. The name's Dyfi, and I'm in year two. Nice to meet you all."

"So what do we do now?" John asked.

"We sit and wait for our instructions," Monix told him. "Lorem goes around to all the teams and tells them what they'll be doing. He does it every year."

"How long's he going to take?" complained Tarope. "I want to get started with the energy weapons!" He slashed his hand through the air. "*Whumm, zumm, zoooo ...*"

"Oh, I imagine he'll be here any moment," said Lorem, suddenly standing in the centre of the group.

John hadn't noticed the headmaster flash up through the floor in his energy-ball form. As much as you saw it happen, the way Lorem could suddenly appear out of nowhere like that was still startling.

There was a low humming sound, and an Examiner glided into the room. John's stomach lurched, but he told himself to stay calm. *I haven't done anything wrong. Well, nothing I know about, anyway ...*

"Every team must have a leader," Lorem explained to the group. "Before I can give you the details of your task, I need you to select who your leader will be. I want you to nominate out loud at least two candidates for leader, then vote for the candidate you prefer."

"How do we vote?" piped Dyfi.

"Just think about your chosen candidate. This Examiner will then scan your minds and announce the winner."

Examiners can scan thoughts? John puzzled. He hadn't known that, and the new knowledge gave him the cold shudders. That made him wonder if the Examiner could tell what he was thinking right then, and that made John feel even worse. He clenched his jaw and tried not to think about it.

"I nominate myself for leader," Monix said firmly. "I'm the oldest, and I've been in more Space Spectaculars than the rest of you, so I know the ropes. It makes sense."

That works for me, John thought. Monix seemed to be looking down on them all a bit, but she obviously knew what she was doing.

"I'm nominating John," Kritta said. "He won the Robot Warriors contest. And everyone knows how brave he is. He'd be a great leader."

That came as a shock. *Me, lead the group?* Plenty of protests rose to John's lips – *I can't, I've got no experience, I'm sure you can do better than me* – but he said none of them aloud.

However, Kritta had forgotten something important, and he needed to set her straight. "I wasn't the only winner," he said modestly. "Kaal was the joint winner along with me. So if I'm being nominated for team leader, he ought to be, too."

Kaal mumbled something and looked down at his clawed feet.

"What was that?" snapped Monix.

"I said, 'no thanks'." Kaal's voice was barely above a whisper. "I don't want to be nominated for leader, but thanks all the same."

"Good," said Monix.

"Suit yourself," Tarope shrugged. "Anyone else?"

There were no volunteers.

"Very well," said Lorem. "Everyone, please think of either Monix or John. And do remember that leadership is an honour as well as a duty."

This is not an easy decision, John reflected. Monix clearly knew what she was doing, but then, leading a team might be fun. He was sure Lorem would think highly of people who stepped up to the job.

I should vote for myself, John thought, and was about to – but then doubt took over.

Am I ready to lead a team? What would I be letting myself in for? It's a lot of responsibility. What if someone makes me look like an idiot in front of everyone's families? I know I can trust Kaal – but what about these others? I barely know them! And Morix WANTS to be leader, so I should let her have the job.

His mind made up, he thought of Monix as the Examiner scanned him with a flickering red beam. Making a satisfied-sounding beep, the Examiner moved the other students. John shivered at the thought of that thing poking about in his brain.

Once all the students had been scanned, the Examiner moved back and paused dramatically. Then it declared in its flat, impassive voice: "SELECTION MADE. LEADER WILL BE STUDENT JOHN RILEY."

"What?"John said before he could stop himself.

Using its manipulator beam, the Examiner passed John a flat, slim digital notepad. "THIS IS YOUR TEAM SHEET. IT CONTAINS IMPORTANT RULES. STUDY IT CAREFULLY."

John looked at the device and passed it Kaal, too awestruck to think straight. They voted for *me*? But working out the maths, that meant the only people to vote for Monix were John and Monix herself! Though she obviously thought he'd voted for himself, by the look of her.

I'm not sure I'm up to this, he thought.

"Well, leader?" Monix said sulkily. "What do you want us to do first?"

"Um ... why don't we all have a look at the team sheet? Let's see what we're meant to be doing." It seemed like a good place to start, John figured.

The team clustered around the little digital notepad, talking excitedly about Laser Pros and Hotshots, whatever they were.

John felt a tap on his shoulder. It was Lorem, who John had forgotten was still here.

"John, might I have a little word?"

"Of course."

Lorem led John off to one side. "I know your parents won't be able to attend the show, for obvious reasons. But don't let that deter you! For the thousands of other parents who can come, you will be their first-ever experience of an Earthling. I am looking forward to seeing you put your planet firmly on their galactic map."

John smiled despite his misgivings. "I'll do my best, I promise."

"I am sure you will. You learn very quickly, John. Indeed, I often forget you are from Earth, and not one of the more advanced planets. If I expect a great deal of you, it is only because you are capable of great things."

"Thanks," John said. He hoped Lorem was right, because at that moment he was not feeling it himself. But the headmaster had given him something to live up to. If his parents couldn't be here, he could at least make Lorem proud.

"Now, if you'll excuse me, I have to brief the Zero-G Acrobatics team. Good luck, Galactic Battle team. And, if you don't mind, please don't blow any holes in the ship. I'm rather fond of it."

Lorem and the Examiner left – one through the floor in energy-ball form, the other through the door – and John gathered the group around the team sheet. A large BRIEFING icon was flashing, so he pressed it.

A fan of laser light beamed upward from the team sheet, forming into a hologram of a smiling, computer-generated figure. She looked like a perky robot cheerleader, wearing a T-shirt and shorts in the team's bright yellow colour.

"Hi, team!" the hologram said. "I'm Ton-3, your personal coach and instructor! You're going to love the task we've set for you. For the Space Spectacular, you're going to defeat a group of Defendroids using three different types of energy weapons! We don't want anyone getting hurt, so you'll have authentic high-impact GalactoFlak battlesuits to wear, too."

"Cool!" said Kritta. And John was glad to see that the rest of the team seemed delighted, too.

Images flashed across the screen of the team sheet – huge, stomping robots that looked grim and unfriendly. John assumed that these were Defendroids.

"Jeepers!" said Ton-3. 'Defendroids are no

picnic! Better get some practice, huh? You're going to need teamwork to bring down those bad boys!" Her cheerleader outfit morphed into a GalactoFlak battlesuit, a close-fitting mesh with moulded armour panels.

"So what are we practising *with*, exactly?" asked Tarope.

From behind her back, Ton-3 produced a sleek, white rod with a lens on one end and a set of controls on the base. "The first weapon you're going to need to show off is the LaserPro! You can collect your LaserPros from the Junkyard in the technology facility. Well, what are you waiting for?"

Maybe this won't be as difficult as I feared, John thought, as the team trooped over to the technology facility. The team seemed keen, and LaserPros looked easy to use. *Perhaps I was getting worked up over nothing ...*

A box of LaserPros was waiting in the storage area the students all called the Junkyard. John picked one up and checked the team sheet.

"Ignite your LaserPro by pressing the red switch," it said. "Make sure the safety toggle is set to ON."

John activated the weapon, and a metre and a half of brilliant energy sprang from the tip. "Wow!" he gasped. He tried a few practice swings.

"Try slicing through that old length of vent pipe," Tarope suggested. "I've heard these things go through metal like zarb-butter!"

John slashed the pipe in half with one blow. The tarnished metal was bright and gleaming where he'd cut through it.

"That is so cool!" he said. "We're going to have to be careful with these, though. Battlesuits on, everyone. I don't want anyone getting their limbs chopped off."

A nasty metallic chuckle came from behind one of the storage racks. G-Vez the Serve-U-Droid popped out its head.

"Indeed," it said smugly. "Robots can be repaired. Human beings aren't so easy to fix, are they?"

"Get lost, G-Vez," said Kaal. "And the same goes for your master, if he's hiding here, too."

"Master has better things to do," the droid said archly. "Now, run along."

John noticed G-Vez was clutching a metal claw.

The annoying little Serve-U-Droid was obviously scavenging spare parts from broken-down droids, left over from the Robot Warriors contest. John wondered why. He was sure that if the droid were broken, Mordant would probably just scrap him and get a new one.

John tried to ignore G-Vez and get back to the task at hand: battlesuits. The team pulled them on. John was amazed that the fabric didn't have even a trace of a seam. He gave one of his armoured panels an experimental punch and felt nothing at all.

The team talked excitedly among themselves as they hurried back to force field 1.0. Even Monix seemed happier now, flipping her LaserPro in her hand and catching it. Kritta kept repeating, "This is the *best* team. Everyone else will be so jealous."

"Good work!" said Ton-3 on their return, swinging a holographic LaserPro around in each of her robotic hands. "Now you're going to need to get some practice in. I can generate some holos for you to fight, but live opponents are better."

"OK, you heard her!" said John. "We'll divide the team into pairs for sparring. Kaal, you fight Monix.

Kritta, pair up with Dyfi. Tarope, spar with me."

As they spread out and ignited their LaserPros, John thought, *They all did what I said, without question. I am a leader, after all! This is going to be easy!*

But that feeling soon evaporated as he saw Tarope fumbling with his ignited LaserPro.

"Hold on," the frog-like alien panted. "I'm just trying to get a good grip."

The trouble was, Tarope's skin was slimy. The harder he tried to grip his LaserPro, the more it slipped out of his grasp like wet soap in the bath. John stood in a fighting stance, feeling a bit ridiculous, but doing his best to be patient.

"OK!" Tarope finally yelled, clutching his LaserPro in both hands. "Got it now. On guard, human! *Yaaaaa!*"

Tarope charged at John on his floppy, froggy legs, swinging his energy blade around his head.

John clumsily brought his own blade up to parry – but he never got the chance. Tarope's LaserPro slipped from his hands and went flying across the room.

Kritta squeaked and ducked, and the LaserPro whizzed through the air where her head had been seconds before. It hit the wall, bounced off with a fizz of energy, landed on the floor, and switched itself off.

"Sorry!" John called over, biting his lip.

Kritta shook her head and tried to carry on duelling with Dyfi, but it was a mess. Dyfi could hardly hold the LaserPro in her tiny hands, and Kritta's extra limbs kept getting in the way. "Eep!" she yelled, as she nearly hit her own leg.

An uncomfortable feeling was beginning to creep into John's mind. Maybe no leader could possibly whip this team into shape. Tarope couldn't keep hold of his LaserPro, Kritta was literally falling over herself, and Dyfi couldn't even lift her weapon. Maybe they were just a team of duds.

I'm the leader. I have to say something.

"OK, Tarope, let's go over that again," he said. "Maybe if you pace yourself a bit? Instead of an all-out attack, try a few cuts and thrusts—"

"Oh, save it," Tarope said angrily. "These stupid things are probably defective." He kicked his turned-off LaserPro across the room, then sat down and gazed over at Monix.

John could see that Monix and Kaal were actually doing pretty well. The floating oblong was able to zip and weave in the air, dodging out of the way of Kaal's swipes, while Kaal himself seemed cool and confident, blocking Monix's sudden lunges.

"At least some of us know what they're doing," Tarope grumbled.

At first John thought Tarope was just admiring their skill, but then he began to wonder. Was Tarope having a dig at *him*?

The thought made him feel miserable. *I'm in way over my head. Monix would have made a much better leader than me.*

From the way Tarope and the others were watching Monix perform, he guessed they were thinking the same thing.

CHAPTER 4

The bell sounded for lunch, and not a moment too soon. John felt ready to collapse.

"All right, everyone. We'll break for lunch in the Centre, then the team sheet says we have to go and meet Master Tronic in the Belly."

"I've never been down to the Belly," Dyfi said, sounding worried. "Is it as scary as everyone says?"

John had no idea, but he didn't want to say so. "Let's sort out our own bellies before we worry about that."

It was a lame joke, but Kritta giggled anyway. As soon as Kaal noticed, he joined in, too. John felt a little better for that. It made him glad to know his friend was trying to cheer him up. He still felt so tired, he could barely face the walk. A whole morning of trying to improve the team's weaponry skills had really taken it out of him. They had practised for hours and hours, with John urging them to change partners, try techniques suggested by the team sheet, and rehearse a few flashy moves that John thought would go down well with the parents.

It wouldn't be so bad if I was any good with the LaserPros myself, John thought glumly. *Kaal and Monix are much better than me. But it's my job to make sure we all put on a good performance. What was it Lorem said? "Every student gets to shine in the Space Spectacular." But how can they shine if I don't get them to shape up?*

"Galactic standard credit for your thoughts?" Kritta said, falling into step beside John and Kaal. Tarope, Monix, and Dyfi lagged behind, talking among themselves.

"Right now, I'm hoping Zepp's arranged something I can actually eat," John said. "He tries his best, but he's still not an expert in making Earth food yet."

Lately, Zepp, Hyperspace High's computer system, had been experimenting with desserts. John had looked forward to the "apple turnover", but to his disappointment had found an upside-down apple on his plate. Even worse, he'd nearly broken his teeth on the Mars bar made from a piece of rock from the planet Mars. Sometimes Zepp could be a bit too literal.

Kritta chatted all the way to the Centre, asking John all about his Robot Warriors victory. It was weird talking to someone with such huge, inhuman eyes who clicked and buzzed between words, but she was very friendly.

Her odd looks didn't seem to bother Kaal; the huge Derrilian was listening to her intently. *He's probably hoping she'll mention his own victory in Robot Warriors*, John thought. He and Kaal had been the first-ever *joint* winners, after all.

"Kritta?" Kaal said, as they entered the Centre. "Do you ... uh ... want to find a table?"

"Sure!" she said. "How about that one? That looks big enough for all of us."

"Oh, yes. *All of us*. That's what I meant."

"Back in a sec, guys," John told them. "I'm going to have a quick look for Emmie."

"Good idea," Kaal said, and sat down next to Kritta.

John looked up and down the huge airy Centre, which had already been returned to its usual look, trying to see Emmie's silver hair among the crowds. She would have been with Mordant Talliver all morning, which meant plenty of chances for him to insult and bully her. John had a troubling suspicion that he'd find her in tears. Maybe she was even hiding in her dorm.

But no – there she was, sitting on her own by the central lake, drinking something pink and foamy through a bendy straw, and looking perfectly fine! *Even better than fine*, John thought. He hurried over to join her.

"Hey!" she said happily. "How's it going? Having fun with Galactic Battle?"

"They made me team leader!"

"No way!" she said, laughing.

"I know. I was amazed, too."

"That's ace! You'll do brilliantly. I know you will."

"Oh, it's early days yet," John said hesitantly.

"We're a bit rough around the edges. Well, OK, we're *very* rough. At least we haven't had to call in the Meteor Medics ... not so far, anyway."

Emmie shuddered. "Don't talk about the Meteor Medics. I'm trying not to think about ending up in the medical wing."

"I thought zero-G acrobatics was safe?"

"It's supposed to be. But check this out. For our Space Spectacular performance, they're projecting a ZeBub the stage. You know what that is, right?"

"A zero-gravity bubble?" John guessed.

"Exactly! And we all get to fling each other around inside it, doing flips and somersaults and mid-air spins and cool stuff like that. Which is fine ... so long as your partner doesn't throw you *out* of the ZeBub. You know, by accident." She gave John a significant look.

John put two and two together. "Your partner wouldn't happen to be Mordant Talliver, would it?"

"He's our team leader," she said, sighing. "So he got to choose." She slurped her drink noisily. "I volunteered as leader, too, but Mordant dropped some nasty hints about 'accidents' that might happen if he wasn't chosen. Nobody wanted to take the risk.

Zero-G acrobatics is dangerous enough!"

John's flesh was crawling at the thought of Emmie's life in Mordant Talliver's hands. "Accidents," Mordant had said. John knew all too well what that could mean. "How's he been with you lately? Is he still acting, you know, weird?"

"That's the part I can't understand!" Emmie whispered. "He's being so *nice*!"

John was about to tell her not to trust Mordant, *especially* if he was acting nice, but he never got the chance. Suddenly Mordant himself was at the table, appearing silently from out of the crowds. G-Vez bobbed along behind him, the obedient servant as always.

"Sorry to butt in," Mordant said with a grin. "Emmie, we need to go. Afternoon practice starts in five minutes, remember? I said only twenty minutes for lunch."

"Oh, no," Emmie said, standing up. "I can't believe it. I lost track of time!"

Mordant patted her arm, which made John's blood pressure skyrocket. He said to her in a smooth voice, "Don't sweat it. I know I'm pushing the team hard. I just want us to wow every single person who comes to watch."

"You're not angry?"

"Of course not. We're on the same team. I've got your back."

"Thanks, Mordant," Emmie said, sounding wary that Mordant's behaviour was too good to be true.

John wanted to ask the half-Gargon where the real Mordant Talliver had gone. Was he tied up in his dorm? Was this some shape-shifting alien that had taken his place?

Mordant turned to go.

Emmie rushed off behind him, calling back over her shoulder. "John? I'll see you and Kaal for dinner later on, yeah?"

"Sure. Later, Emmie."

What Emmie had told John had begun to prey on his mind. Emmie's life in Mordant's hands? John already knew that was going to keep John awake at night. There were so many different ways Mordant could hurt her in zero-G acrobatics, and Emmie was right – it would be easy to make it look like an accident, even with everyone watching. John clenched his fist, thinking of what he'd do if Mordant hurt his friend.

But physical injury wasn't really Mordant's style. And anyway, he'd had plenty of chances to hurt Emmie already but hadn't. Mordant could usually be counted on to make some snarky comment or other, mocking her for being slow in class. But by the sound of it, he'd been polite. Better than polite. He'd been *nice*.

"Stop stressing," John said to himself. "He's just buttering her up because he's team leader and he wants everyone's support, that's all. You've got nothing to worry about."

John made his way back to where Kaal and Kritta were sitting. Tarope, Monix, and Dyfi had joined them, and they were all eating Blargon burgers with Pepperdust fries. The Blargon burgers quivered like rubber, and they squeaked like dog toys when you bit into them.

Kritta was in the middle of gossiping with Dyfi when John arrived. "Can you believe it? That claw-varnish cost Shazilda *stacks* of credit—" She broke off when she spotted John. "Hi, John, I saved you a chair!" then she turned back to Dyfi. "And Ms Skrinel just confiscated it in front of everyone! I know it glows pretty bright and Shaz shouldn't have been putting it on in class, but seriously, how harsh is that?"

"Totally," Dyfi said. "Hey, Kaal, are you going to eat that?"

"Hmm?" said Kaal dreamily. His Blargon burger lay untouched in front of him, and only a few of his Pepperdust fries had been eaten. He was staring at Kritta as if she'd hypnotized him. *What was going on?* It dawned on John that Derrilians *ate* insects. This could be bad. It would really mess things up if Kaal couldn't help seeing Kritta as a huge Sunday roast. He was sure the rules didn't allow one team member to eat another!

John quickly gobbled down a delicious jacket potato with cheese and beans. He had to admit, Zepp had made his lunch perfectly. The cheese was melted just right, the butter was soft and golden, the beans were luscious, and the potato was not even wearing a little dinner jacket!

"We'd better get going," Monix said. She sounded so sure of herself, John thought, anyone would think she was the leader.

Kaal left the table, carrying his barely touched

lunch with him, and went to empty his tray into the auto-recycle machines. As soon as he was gone, Kritta leaned over the table and whispered to John, "I've got a confession to make. Don't be mad, OK?"

"Um ... really?" was all John could think of to say.

"I'm a huge fan of yours," Kritta clicked. "Like, really huge. Ever since Robot Warriors. I'm so glad we're on the same team! It means we can spend much more time together."

Before she could say anything else, Kaal returned and they all headed out of the Centre together. John's thoughts were in a whirl. He couldn't help feeling he was missing something obvious, something he'd kick himself over later. But right now, this felt like yet one more expectation to live up to.

Great. Kritta's a big fan, and now I get to be her team leader. No pressure there, then ...

"How do we get to the Belly, anyway?" Dyfi asked, still sounding uncertain about the whole trip.

John activated Ton-3, who sprung up from the team sheet immediately. She was wearing a helmet with a lamp on it.

"To access the Belly, take service lift sixty-eight

down to level minus four," she explained. "Then follow the corridor straight ahead until you reach the holding cell where the Defendroids are kept. You can't miss it!"

"*Service lift?*" said Kritta. "Ew."

John stopped outside a pair of grey, industrial-looking sliding doors. "Um. I think we're here, guys."

"Are you sure that's not the waste compactor?" Monix asked.

John pressed the big yellow button beside the doors, and they hissed open to reveal a cramped metal interior. "It looks like a lift to me."

"Let's hope so," Tarope said darkly. "Those would be rubbish last words."

"How are we all going to fit in there?" Monix complained. "Can't we go down separately, in two elevators, one after another?"

"No!" yelped Dyfi. "All together, or I'm not going! We don't know what's down there waiting for us in the Belly, and I've heard some nasty rumours."

"Strength in numbers," said Kritta. "She's got a point."

"OK," John sighed, sure that Dyfi was just getting

worked up over nothing. "Let's do this."

Getting everyone in took a *lot* of squeezing and shuffling. In the end, Kaal was wedged in a corner, Monix hovered by the ceiling, Dyfi cowered on the floor in the middle of everyone, Tarope was jammed against Kaal's left wing, and Kritta was pressed up so uncomfortably close to John that his chin was on top of her head.

He pressed the button for level minus four, and the lift trundled down into the darkness. Nobody spoke. The lights on the lift panel steadily ticked down, reaching the main level, numbered zero – and then down even further.

From somewhere below came a sudden metallic screech. Kritta gasped, and Dyfi made a frightened peeping noise.

"That was just the lift," Tarope said, sounding like he wanted to believe it.

All too soon, the doors hissed open.

After the tight, cramped lift, the huge open tunnels of the Belly were a surprise. *It's almost like a cathedral*, John thought; great steely pillars rose into unseen heights, and shafts of dim light broke the gloom. But it was all too easy to imagine sinister figures lurking high in the shadows, waiting to pounce.

Up above, a tiny hovering shape ducked quickly out of sight. In a flash of silver it was gone. *A bat? Don't be daft, Riley. This is a spaceship, not Dracula's castle!* John tried to assure himself.

"What *is* this place?" Dyfi said.

"Storage, mostly," said Monix. "This is where the droids live, out of sight of the rest of the ship."

"I'm not scared of a few old robots," muttered Tarope. But then something made the loud sound of a rattling chain, and he gave a sudden little croak of fear.

"Defendroids aren't robots like you're used to," Monix said. "They're dangerous. Like guard beasts."

"Right," John said, feeling like he had to call things to order. "Ton-3 said to go this way."

"Are you sure?" Kritta said nervously. "This way doesn't look very welcoming."

John referred to the team sheet again, and the hologram of Ton-3 flashed up before them. "That is correct. But take care, Galactic Battle team," she said mysteriously before disappearing again.

Right on cue, a low mechanical growl came from the shadows. There was the sound of metal scraping against metal.

Kritta grabbed hold of John's arm and clung to him tightly. "I really don't want to be here."

Kaal reached out for Kritta's other arm. "It's OK, Kritta," he said. "This pair of Robot Warrior champions won't let anything hurt you."

"Come on, everyone," John insisted. "Let's not get too worked up over this, eh?" But in spite of his words, his own heart was beating fast as he led them through the dark tunnels. If the robots were as scary as they sounded, he wasn't sure he wanted to meet them face to face.

As the group turned a corner, John glimpsed a skeletal robot form looming through the shadows. A sinister red light pulsed from its gleaming metal skull.

It turned to face the group and began to run towards them in a lurching stride ...

CHAPTER 5

Dyfi squeaked and hid behind John's leg.

"It's OK!" John said. "It's only Master Tronic, here to meet us already. See?"

"Oh," Dyfi said, poking her head out. "Sorry, sir. You gave me a bit of a scare."

"Think nothing of it," Master Tronic said. "I'm used to the students not recognizing me at first."

John understood what he meant. The technology teacher changed his body to suit whatever he was teaching. Right now, he was a lean robot with four tool-tipped arms, perfect for teaching electronic maintenance and repair. The only thing that never changed was the red light beam from his head.

"So, Galactic Battle team," said Master Tronic, "are you ready to meet the Defendroids? There are six of them, which is why this team is limited to six students."

He gestured behind him to a large reinforced window, behind which several huge shadowy shapes paced back and forth in near-darkness. They looked twice as tall as Master Tronic. Mechanical roars and snarls came from within. The door beside the window looked like it could withstand a nuclear missile strike.

John and the others looked at each other nervously.

"Well, don't all charge forward at once," Master Tronic said, his voice heavy with synthetic sarcasm. "Come on, team. You need to get a proper look at them while they're in full aggression mode. I don't want you to forget what you're dealing with."

I guess this is where the leader has to set the example, John thought. *Nobody wants to be first. Even Monix looks worried. But if I don't go, nobody will.*

John stepped forward, walking slowly until he was right in front of the window. Kritta followed behind, then all the others. The Defendroids inside were still hard to see in the dark, but John saw an enormous metal claw brush by the window, and his heart thumped painfully in his chest.

"That's better," said Master Tronic. "And now ..." He flipped open a control panel next to the window and pressed a switch. Instantly, light flooded the room inside.

Everyone gasped, including John.

The six Defendroids were roughly human-shaped, but they each had two arms: one ending in a spiked, lumpy sphere and the other in a long curved blade. Their faces looked like they were full of brute anger, with big jutting chins and tiny little red eyes.

"Technically, they're called DF-221 to DF-226," said Master Tronic, "but I have my own names for them. Basher, Lasher, Slicer, Dicer, Crusher, and Steel Storm."

"Cute names!" John said sarcastically.

The Defendroids stomped back and forth, swivelling their heads to the left and right – and sometimes, frighteningly, all the way around to face in the other direction. When they did that, their arms and legs rotated in their sockets to match the direction of their head, and the robot stomped off back the way it had come, without having to turn around.

From time to time, the robots would roar and bash the ground or the walls, sending a tremor through the floor. It was as if they had to attack , or they would go crazy from imprisonment.

"As you can see," Master Tronic said, "they are heavily armed. One wrecking ball arm, one blade arm with extendable circular saw. They can stamp with the force of a pile driver, electrify their limbs, and even extend the wrecking ball on a chain to ensnare their opponents."

"I'm not sure if that's the scariest thing I've ever seen, or the coolest," Tarope said.

"Why are these things called Defendroids?" Kritta asked. "The way they're acting, shouldn't they be Attackdroids or something?"

"These beauties are part of the school's defence system," Master Tronic explained proudly. "Right now they're in full aggression mode. We keep them that way when they're in storage, because if the school was ever attacked, they'd need to be sent in to fight

73

the intruders right away."

"We can't fight them, even with LaserPros!" Monix complained. "They'll crush us to a pulp!"

"We didn't invite the entire school's parents to Hyperspace High to watch their children go *splat*," Master Tronic said. "Pay attention, all of you. Whenever you use the Defendroids to spar with, you have to switch them over to training mode. Like this."

Master Tronic pressed a sequence of keys on the control panel at the door and a peculiar blue pulsing light began to ripple through the cell. The Defendroids stopped their constant stomping and stood still, arms hanging by their sides. Without the roaring and crashing, it was suddenly deathly quiet.

"They'll still fight, of course," Master Tronic said, "but it's strictly non-lethal. Oh, they'll put on a good show, but the chances of anyone actually getting injured are very slim indeed."

"Well, that's good to know," Monix said in an icy tone.

Master Tronic ignored her. "John, the passcode to put the robots in training mode is SOMNOLA, and the code to set them back to full aggression mode is

LEXTALIONIS. Don't ever, *ever* open this door without entering the training code first. Not unless you want to spend the Space Spectacular in the medical wing!"

"Got the message loud and clear, sir," John said, committing the codes to memory. "Thanks." Out of the corner of his eye, he saw something zip away in the upper shadows. The flying thing again! Or was he seeing things?

Master Tronic activated another control, and the great door groaned open with a hiss of pistons. "In you go, then. They're set to follow your voice commands."

Despite everything Master Tronic had said about the Defendroids being safe now, John hesitated. He *really* didn't want to go in there. But the team needed him. He forced himself to walk in.

"Come on, you lot," he said to the silent Defendroids. "Follow me. It's time for energy weapon practice."

"CONFIRMED," said the nearest Defendroid, in a voice that grated like rusty metal.

Kritta was staring at John with her mouth open. "You just walked right in. Wow. That was so cool."

"Just one problem," Kaal said. "Where are we going to practise? We can't go back to force field on point zero. It will be too crowded."

"We'd be less likely to hit each other if we had a bit more room," said Kritta tactfully.

"I suggest you use the Sonic Sports Hall," Master Tronic said. "And you'd better head up in the Grav-Lifter beam, too. You'll never get the Defendroids in a service lift."

"No kidding. We barely got *us* in a service lift," Monix grumbled.

"So what is the Grav-Lifter beam exactly?" John asked the team sheet as they walked on through the Belly corridors, the Defendroids in training mode following close behind.

Ton-3 flashed into being. She had changed outfits again. Now she was wearing a workman's vest and holding a mag-spanner. "It's for hauling the big loads between decks! No need for platforms or lifts – just a big, wide open shaft, with tractor beams to pull you up or down!"

"Uh oh," said Tarope. Up ahead lay the edge of what looked like a gaping circular pit, easily twenty metres across. "I think this must be it."

A faint reddish light pulsed down the length of the shaft.

John gulped. "Do we just ... walk over the edge?"

"You got it!" chirped Ton-3.

"I'll go first," Kaal said boldly, striding in front. His wings twitched, ready to bear him up, if need be. He took a step over the edge and hung there in space, the edges of his body glowing in the beam.

"OK, everyone," John said. "All together, on the count of three. One, two ... three!"

Together, they walked over the edge. Kritta held her hands over her eyes. Suddenly, John felt like he was walking on soft pillows. He looked down, and immediately wished he hadn't. The shaft seemed to drop down to infinity.

"We're moving!" Tarope said.

Sure enough, the whole team, Defendroids and all, was rising steadily upward.

John could see the bright lights of the ship's upper decks shining far above. He kept his eyes fixed on that, refusing to look down again.

When the Galactic Battle team reached the Sonic

Sports Hall, John still felt more than a little giddy from his ride on the Grav-Lifter beam. Being hauled up through several decks without even a platform to stand on had been a bit nerve-wracking, to say the least.

Still, the admiring glances and comments they'd got from the other students as they'd departed the Grav-Lifter beam and led the Defendroids through the corridors to the Sonic Space Hall had been worth it. John was feeling almost proud of them now.

He activated the touchscreen outside the hall. "OK, team. We can customize the room for Galactic Battle, and there are loads of options. Random floor tilt, laser turret fire, maze settings, reflectors ..."

The team looked at him with expressions of horror.

"Or I could just set it to basic," he added hastily. "Simple, shock-resistant and soundproof. Yeah. I think we'll go for basic."

"Good choice," Kritta whispered as they filed inside.

"This looks great!" said Tarope, running into the centre of the hall. "There's loads of room."

"OK, everyone!" John called. "Ready to get some

serious practice in?"

Everyone except Monix yelled, "Yeah!"

Monix just shrugged, which looked pretty weird on a floating oblong.

"So how does this work?" Kritta asked. "We can't actually damage the Defendroids permanently, can we?"

Ton-3 was quick to answer, now back and wearing her bright-yellow team T-short and shorts. "When your weapons have their safety on, they won't do any permanent damage. The Defendroids will count how many times you've successfully hit them. Twenty hits and they fall over until the next round. Oh, and bashing them on the head is a critical hit and stuns them. If you can manage it."

Just like fighting a goblin in the World of Khaos video game, John thought.

"And what do we do when they hit us?" Monix said acidly. "Bleed on them?"

"They won't hit us," John assured her. "In training mode, they back off when they're hit."

"That's a relief," said Dyfi. "Otherwise, we'd all be squished!"

"OK, team, let's get to work," John said. "This morning was a bit of a shambles, but never mind, that's all behind us. We've got proper opponents now, so we can really cut loose. First, everyone spread out and find a space."

The team did as he asked – except Monix, who stayed where she was. *She's really sore about not being leader*, John thought to himself. *I mustn't let it get to me.* But it still stung to have her ignore him so obviously.

"Defendroids!" he yelled. "Each one of you, pick an opponent!"

Steel Storm, Basher, Lasher, Slicer, Dicer, and Crusher stomped into position, matching themselves against the team members.

"OK, team," John said, "It's game on. Fight!"

The LaserPros flared into life, and instantly the hall was full of the din of energy beams clashing and sparking off robust robot bodies. The Defendroids attacked slowly, giving their opponents plenty of time to dodge, and the LaserPros looked awesome as they slashed brightly through the air.

We can do this, John thought. *All we needed was*

a bit more space!

But although the team was less scrappy than before, they were still only swiping at the Defendroids back and forth. Every time they seemed to gain some ground, the robots drove them back again. John needed to change strategy.

"Let's form a circle, everyone! Stand side by side, and let the robots come at us. We can guard each other's backs!"

Dyfi and Tarope began to back towards him, but Kaal seemed to be in a world of his own. He was talking to Kritta – or trying to.

"I heard you liked Robot Warriors," John heard him say. "You know I was joint champion, right?"

"Yeah," Kritta said, blocking Lasher's snaking whip with her LaserPro.

"I could show you my blueprints if you like, I've still got them …"

"Huh?" Kritta said. "Sorry, did you say something?"

John turned away, frustrated. Why wasn't Kaal concentrating on the task at hand? Where was Monix?

Then he saw her, swinging her LaserPro wildly.

One slash narrowly missed Kaal's wingtip. Another thwacked Kritta on the upper arm.

"Hey! Watch it!" Kritta shouted. "If your safety hadn't been on, you'd have sliced my arm off!"

"Monix, try to keep your attacks focused!" John called.

"I know what I'm doing!" she shouted at him. She was battering Basher mercilessly, driving it across the room. "You should be watching my moves instead of trying to order me about!"

Basher was backing away from her furious attacks. But it took John a second to notice that it was stomping right towards him.

Suddenly, as if it sensed an easier target, Basher whizzed its head round. Then its arms and legs. It struck out at John with its wrecking-ball arm. In a reflex action, John whacked away the ball – with milliseconds to spare.

But now Basher was on him, slamming and swiping. Never mind what Master Tronic had said – those swinging limbs looked dangerous! *Had Monix driven the Defendroid into him on purpose?*

John struck desperately at the Defendroid with his

LaserPro, scoring minor hits here and there. Where on earth was the rest of his team? He looked around, and saw them watching the fight. They just stood there waiting for orders, staring gormlessly as if they were watching holo-TV, unsure of what to do next.

"A little help?" John yelled.

Kaal began to edge forward, glancing back at Kritta, but just as that moment, one of John's wild blows connected with Basher's head. Its eyes flashed, registering a the critical hit, and it sank slowly to the floor.

John switched off his LaserPro and stood, breathing heavily.

"I've had more than enough of this for one day," he said. He knew he sounded frustrated and worn out, but right now he just didn't care. "I'm going to take the Defendroids back to their cell. We'll meet up here again tomorrow morning, nine sharp. Let's all get some rest. Don't worry. I'm sure things will go better tomorrow."

They could hardly go any worse, he thought, and turned to leave.

CHAPTER 6

"This just doesn't feel right," John said. "I wish I knew where Emmie was."

John and Kaal were sitting together in the Centre, at a table made from translucent black material with swirling holographic lights dancing in it.

"Oh, she can take care of herself," Kaal said, waving a dismissive hand. "Hey, what snacks do you think Kritta likes? Felgercrunchies? Or would they make her explode? I could try running an experiment in the labs, but I'd need some of her DNA ..."

The scampi and chips Zepp had made for John were delicious – golden, crisp, and just salty enough

– but two things were spoiling his dinner.

One was Emmie, or rather, the *lack* of Emmie. She'd said she would meet them for dinner, but she was nowhere to be seen.

The other was Kaal, who had finally plucked up the courage to try more of John's food, but was instead dissecting every little bit and arranging the fragments on the table in front of him. It reminded John of how he used to eat Jaffa Cakes when he was little, nibbling off the edge and devouring the orange bit last.

"Fascinating," Kaal commented, as he unwrapped the batter on a piece of scampi. "The little dead sea creatures are all encased in this brittle stuff. It's like they're entombed." He added the pieces to his growing collection.

"You're supposed to just eat it," John said. "It's not good manners to take your dinner to bits."

"But I'm learning about it!" Kaal protested. "This Earth food is just so weird. Crawly sea creatures and tubers from under the ground, on the same dish?"

"I told you, all you have to do is ask me about it. You don't have to pick the food apart!"

Kaal folded his arms and made a stubborn face.

"How else do you learn except by taking things apart? That's science!"

"You can't look at everything as if it were a science problem, Kaal. Even if you are a boffin."

Kaal looked across at where Kritta was sitting and heaved a long sigh. "Maybe you're right. Maybe sometimes, you need to go with your feelings instead of using logic ..."

John wondered what on Earth Kaal's feelings could possibly have to do with his dissected scampi. "It's just about good manners," he tried to say, but Kaal didn't seem to be listening.

Kritta was at a nearby table along with her friends, Shazilda the purple horned girl, and Dol, the dolphin-like P'Sidion who wore a bubble-shaped helmet filled with water. They were talking among themselves, giggling at some shared joke.

All the way through his meal, Kaal had been staring at Kritta, obviously trying to puzzle something out. It was so frustrating. Talking to Kaal about anything important right now was like trying to communicate with a raw potato.

Suddenly, Emmie was there, shoving her way

through the tables to reach them. John stood up happily, but the smile faded from his face as soon as he saw hers. Her navy-blue eyes were brimming with blue tears, and she looked furious.

"Emmie?" he said.

She folded her arms and looked from John to Kaal and back. "Thanks. Thanks ever so much for the present. You really shouldn't have."

John's brain went into a confused wheel spin. Kaal just frowned a little, as if Emmie's outburst meant nothing to him.

"Wha-what are you talking about?" John managed to blurt out.

She wiped her eyes with the back of her hand. "Oh, that's cute. Act like you don't know. Honestly, why don't the two of you just ... just *grow up*?" She threw her arms up in frustration, turned on her heels, and stormed off.

"Emmie, wait!" John called after her. But she was already vanishing through the far doors and away down the hall.

"I think she's upset," Kaal mused.

"Full marks for observation!" John said, sitting

down heavily. "What do you think we've done?"

Kaal shrugged. He had resumed looking at Kritta's table.

"We should go after her," John said. "She's obviously got the wrong end of the stick about something. Maybe she's upset with me about the detention? But she seemed OK about it before ..."

"It might be better to let her calm down a bit first," Kaal suggested. "I'm going to go and join Kritta. Coming?"

John shook his head. "I need to think this over and figure out what Emmie's so angry about." He sat and chewed morosely on a chip, as Kaal strode over to Kritta and her friends. *What's he up to?* John thought. He suddenly had a feeling that whatever Kaal was about to do, it was something stupid.

Kritta glanced up as the big Derrilian approached. "Oh, hi, Kaal. Want to sit down? Where's John? Is he not with you?"

"Thought the two of them were inseparable!" chuckled Shazilda.

As John watched, he had the horrible feeling of watching a train crash in slow motion, and being unable to do anything about it.

But Kaal didn't sit down. Instead, to John's horror, he spread his wings and launched himself into the air, soaring above the startled Kritta. Then he swooped majestically through the air, gliding around her table in a perfect circle.

John covered his face with his hands and then peeped through his fingers. It was like a nightmare. He couldn't look away. It was clear that however stupid he looked, Kaal was trying to make an impression on Kritta. *So that's why he's been acting so weird*, John realized. *He* likes *Kritta!*

Kaal flew around and around, flying in circles above Kritta's table. Kritta, Shazilda, and Dol all gawped up at him in shock.

"What is he doing?" exclaimed Dol. As Kaal flew past again, she gave a frightened squeak and dived under the table.

Kritta and Shazilda just stared in disbelief, and now more and more students in the Centre were staring, too. Some laughed, some pointed, and a few began to record holovids on their ThinScreens.

Great, thought John. *He'll never live this down ...*

What is the big guy doing, flying in circles like a vulture waiting to dive? Kaal's face looked purposeful and deeply serious, as if he were doing something that mattered to him a lot. But that just made him look even more ridiculous.

Half the Centre was laughing at him now. "He's going to start bombing you in a minute!" someone yelled.

"If this is meant to impress Kritta," John muttered under his breath, "you've seriously blown it, mate. This is painful."

Kaal seemed to be waiting for something to happen, but it just wasn't. His face took on a look of desperation as he flew in yet another circle, beating his wings madly.

Eventually, to the whoops and cheers of the watching students, he flew back down to the ground. Looking limp and dejected, he shuffled back to John's table.

John badly wanted to get up and leave, but Kaal was his friend, and John knew you don't run out on your friends. Even if they act like total idiots in front of half the school.

Kaal sat down and buried his face in his hands.

John heard giggling from Kritta's table. She and her friends were whispering behind their hands, pointing and laughing crazily. He caught the words "... maybe they're all like that where he comes from!" and hoped it wasn't Kritta who had said it.

"So much for going with your feelings!" Kaal said, his voice muffled by his huge hands. "That was a total disaster."

"Oh, come on, it can't be all that bad," John said, trying to find the right words. "I'm sure she ... er ... appreciated whatever it was you were trying to do." He paused. "What *were* you trying to do?"

"Don't you have the Wakan-Dothak on your planet?" Kaal asked, lowering his hands. "I thought all worlds had it, or something like it?"

John looked blank.

"It's a mating display," Kaal said, his cheeks an even deeper green with embarrassment. "The Derrilian males fly above the females, and ... ah ... show off how big and strong their wings are."

"Oh," said John. "Oh. I think I get it." *Don't laugh, don't laugh, DON'T LAUGH,* he told himself.

"We prove our strength and agility by flying in perfect circles, so the females know what worthy mates we will ... make ..." His voice trailed off.

"Do you mean to tell me," John said very slowly, "that where you come from, flying about over a girl's head is *flirting*?"

Kaal gave a miserable nod. "I thought it would be so simple," he said sadly. "My parents always told me my Wakan-Dothak would be irresistible, once I was old enough to go and find a girlfriend. Well, Kritta certainly looks like she resisted it!"

"Don't worry, mate," John said, punching Kaal affectionately in the shoulder. "Plenty more fish in the sea, eh?"

"I don't want to date a fish," Kaal said gloomily. "I like Kritta. But she obviously doesn't like me."

John wondered what he could do to snap his friend out of this glum mood. Emmie would have known just what to do. She was brilliant at cheering people up.

That gave him an idea. "Come on. Let's search this ship top to bottom until we find Emmie. If we've done something to upset her, we need to know what it is."

Kaal thought for a second. "You're right," he said.

"No point sitting around and moping. Let's go."

At least that worked, John thought.

So the search began. John and Kaal rode the TravelTube up and down Hyperspace High, hunting for any sign of Emmie. She wasn't in the Zero-Gravity Sports Hall, where students wearing jetpacks were in the middle of an intense game of seven-a-side Ricochet (John thought it looked a lot like basketball, except shots had to be bounced off the walls, floor, or ceiling).

They checked the sprawling Junkyard, where salvaged technology lay in piles and spilled from trays, waiting for Master Tronic to sort it. They explored the Holo Auditorium, which was empty and unnervingly silent when it wasn't full of students in an assembly, and the Library zones, which were crowded with students trying to fit in regular study between practising for the Space Spectacular. Emmie was nowhere to be found.

"Of course!" John said, snapping his fingers. "She'll be in the hangar bay!"

But she wasn't, and Sergeant Jegger, the gruff three-legged Space Flight teacher, told them he hadn't seen her since she'd taken the new t-dart out for a spin. Suddenly a nasty thought came to John – what if Mordant's talk of "accidents" had been more than an idle threat? There was one place they needed to rule out right away, and John hoped against hope that he *wouldn't* find her there.

"But we do have to check," he told Kaal. "She'd do the same for us. You know she would."

And so they rode the TravelTube to the very top of the ship, to the medical wing, where the Meteor Medics hovered back and forth tending to sick or injured students.

But Dr Kasaria, Hyperspace High's doctor, shook her head. "Emmie Tarz? She's not here, boys. What's wrong? Has she had an accident?"

"I was hoping you'd be able to tell us," John said. "I guess no news is good news. Thanks for checking."

"This is getting us nowhere!" Kaal groaned as they headed back down. "Nobody's seen Emmie. I wonder where Mordant is, for that matter!"

"I guess we'd better call it a night," John said, yawning. "At least we know she hasn't been injured. Maybe she'll be in a better mood tomorrow."

"Let's get to the dorm, then – wait! Is that who I think it is?"

The TravelTube's doors had opened, to reveal a familiar Serve-U-Droid, caught in the act of taking a foil packet from one of the corridor wall dispensers.

"There you go, G-Vez," trilled Zepp's voice from the dispenser's speaker. "Thanks for your order!"

G-Vez tried to hide the packet behind its little bulbous back, but John had already seen what was written on it.

"Yoko beans!" he exclaimed. "That's Emmie's favourite snack!"

"Looks like someone's trying to win her over," Kaal said darkly, "and I think we both know who!"

"Are those beans for Emmie?" John demanded.

"I'm not telling," G-Vez snapped. "Out of my way."

"No. Not until you tell us where Emmie is!"

John moved to bar the way. G-Vez hovered for a moment, then suddenly shot between his knees and whizzed off down the hall, letting out an electronic raspberry as he went.

"I can't stand that droid," Kaal muttered.

"There's only one more thing we can do," John

said firmly. "We'll have to send her a Zip."

"Are you sure?" Kaal said, uncertain. "Zip Messages get projected in the air in front of you, no matter where you are or what you're doing. What if she's with a teacher or something? This might make it worse."

"I don't think we have much choice," John said miserably. "Besides, we're already in her bad books. This could be our only chance to make things right. Zepp, I need to send a Zip Message."

"Ready to take your message," Zepp said, still speaking through the snack machine. "What do you want it to say?"

John thought for a moment. "Emmie, what's wrong? Kaal and I have no idea what we did. We need to talk. Come to our dorm as soon as possible. John and Kaal."

And now, John thought, *I need to lie down before I fall over from exhaustion.*

But Emmie's tearful rage was still filling his thoughts. Sleep would be a long way off yet.

CHAPTER 7

John woke to the sound of Zepp humming.

"Huh?" he said, sitting up and rubbing his eyes. "Whazzat?"

"Good morning, John," Zepp said. "If you look directly above your bed, you'll see a Zip Message."

John was instantly wide awake. "From Emmie?"

"That's correct."

John rubbed his eyes again and looked at the holographic letters scrolling above his bed, like an advertising marquee in laser-light.

JOHN AND KAAL. DON'T PLAY ALL INNOCENT WITH ME. YOU KNOW FULL WELL WHAT YOU DID. YOUR STUNT COULD HAVE LANDED ME IN THE

MEDICAL WING. WHAT'S WRONG WITH YOU? DO YOU WANT TO SPEND SPACE SPECTACULAR IN DETENTION? I'M BUSY WITH MY TEAM. BACK OFF AND DON'T BOTHER ME AGAIN.

John felt as if someone had emptied a cold bucket of water over him. "That's it?"

"I'm afraid so. No attachments, no other messages. Sorry if it wasn't what you wanted."

"Not your fault, Zepp. Thanks anyway."

Troubled thoughts raced through John's mind as he dressed. "Stunt? Land her in the medical wing?" he said to himself. "How could she ever think we'd want to do that? I know she takes her zero-G acrobatics seriously, but this is way over the top!"

Mordant must have poisoned her mind against us somehow, he thought – and if there was one thing the half-Gargon boy was good at, it was competitiveness. John had thought the Galactic Battle team, Zero-G Acrobatics team, and all the other teams were all on the same side, and everyone would get a chance to shine at the Space Spectacular. But now Mordant was trying to make it all about one-upmanship and my-team's-better-than-yours.

John punched his pillow angrily. "She's my friend, you slimy git! Leave her alone!"

Kaal wandered out of the bathroom. "Are you having a fight with your bed?"

"Just wishing it was Mordant's face," John grumbled. "Listen to this ..." And he told Kaal about the message.

"But we're friends!" Kaal said, looking hurt. "She couldn't possibly believe we'd hurt her on purpose – could she?"

"She sounds pretty convinced to me."

"I wish we could speak to her," Kaal sighed. "We could talk it through, sort it all out."

"Me, too," John said. "But we haven't got time to chase her down now. We need to practise."

Do we ever, he thought, as he activated the team sheet. *The team needs all the practice it can get. Tomorrow all the families will be arriving for the Space Spectacular, and we're still a total mess.*

"So what are we practising with today?" Kaal asked. "LaserPros again, I hope?"

"No, the team sheet says we're meant to use something called SonicArrows. Look."

The screen showed a holo-image of a slender, platinum-coloured spear, covered with the imprint of fine circuitry. It began to vibrate, its entire length becoming a blur.

"Looks more like a SonicJavelin," Kaal said uneasily. "How do they work?"

John clicked on the HELP icon, and Ton-3 appeared, holding one of the weapons. "The SonicArrow is one of the coolest weapons ever invented, an energy weapon that takes the ancient technology of the spear to new heights! Like the old-fashioned spear, it has to be thrown by hand, but once in the air, it flies using the power of refluxing diatronic sound waves, which are so high-pitched, you can't hear a thing! SonicArrows speed up after they are thrown, so be careful where you launch them."

"That does sound pretty cool," John said. "So you just pick them up and lob them at the target?"

"It's not as simple as that!" said Ton-3, wagging a cautionary finger. "SonicArrows have to be thrown in a single steady movement, so they do not wobble down their length. A wobbling SonicArrow is bad news!"

"Why?" Kaal asked, suddenly looking very worried.

"It sets up a feedback wave in the SonicArrow's flight path. And it sounds like *this*."

The screech that came out of the team sheet made John's knees wobble. It sounded like a cat eating a chilli pepper while dragging its claws down a blackboard.

"Urrgh," he said, turning off the sound. "OK, I get it. If we throw them properly, we can't hear them flying, but if we muck it up, they burst our eardrums." *That should encourage the team to learn pretty quick,* he thought.

"Come on, Kaal. It's nearly nine. Let's go and meet the others."

"Do you think Kritta is still speaking to me?" Kaal asked. "After yesterday?"

"Of course she is," John reassured him. "We're all part of a team!" He really hoped that what he was saying was true.

Kaal paused as they left the dorm. "Did you get oil on your hands down in the Belly last night?"

"No, I don't think so. Why?"

Kaal pointed at their dorm door. There were

smudgy, oily handprints around the control panel. "I guess one of us must have got mucky and not noticed," he mused.

They met the rest of the team in the Sonic Sports Hall (*It will certainly deserve that name today*, John thought), which had been reconfigured to a new shape. Instead of yesterday's wide-open arena, it was now a long narrow hall like a corridor. At the far end loomed the shapes of six Defendroids, but these ones weren't made from metal. They were flat plastic-looking targets, with little point values marked on their body parts in glowing numerals, like archery targets.

John saw a row of SonicArrows lined up in a rack on the wall. Obviously Zepp had arranged the room for them before they even got here. Monix and the others were looking warily at the SonicArrows, clearly unsure what to make of them.

I'd better give them a demonstration, John thought.

"Morning, team! As you can see, we'll be using SonicArrows today. You're probably wondering how they work."

Feeling confident, John grabbed one of the slender

shafts. It felt as light as a soap bubble and as flexible as a length of bamboo. "It's very simple. All you have to do is pick one up, take aim, and throw!"

He flung the SonicArrow as hard as he could. As it left his hand, it wobbled.

An ear-piercing shriek rang out from the flying arrow. The members of the Galactic Battle team covered their ears and made pained faces.

John's arrow thwacked into the wall, a good three metres away from the target he'd meant to hit, before falling with a clatter.

"… taking care not to do *that*, of course." He tried to laugh it off. "As you've just seen, you have to throw a SonicArrow just right, or it'll wobble about and make a horrible noise. Here, watch how I do it this time."

He went and fetched the SonicArrow, took a deep breath, and aimed. He flung it. And again, the same awful noise tore through the air. Again, he missed the target completely.

"Thanks, John. I think we all know how *not* to do it by now," Monix said coldly.

John shrugged while going to collect the SonicArrow. "Just because I'm team leader doesn't mean I'm perfect!"

"You can say *that* again," muttered Monix.

"OK, why doesn't someone else have a go?" John said. "How about you, Kritta?"

"I thought you'd never ask." She smiled.

Kritta gently took the SonicArrow from John's hand, then spun on the spot and threw it with blinding speed, straight at the target.

The arrow struck home, quivering in the Defendroid target's head. Its entire flight had been utterly silent and so fast, it almost seemed to teleport there.

"Wowsers," John said, impressed. "You're a natural!"

"I was the champion under-twelves' Stingshot thrower back on Hive-Seventeen," Kritta admitted. "SonicArrows are a lot like Stingshots. Except less venomous. And more sonic."

"OK, team, change of plan. Kritta's going to teach you all how to throw a Sonicarrow! If that's OK with you, Kritta?"

"It'll be my pleasure," she said, batting her multifaceted eyes at him. Kaal shot John a jealous look.

"It's not my fault," John whispered to him as the

rest of the team lined up. "I haven't done anything to encourage her!"

"I know," Kaal sighed. "I just wish she'd look at me like that, that's all. Just once …"

"All right, listen up!" Kritta yelled. "We're going to start with the throwing stance. Hold your SonicArrow like *this* …"

Half an hour later, John was wishing he'd popped to the Junkyard to borrow some ear protectors. Hardly any member of the team could get the knack of throwing a SonicArrow properly. The noise was horrendous. Screeches, squeals, and screams echoed off the walls as arrow after arrow wobbled through the air. A rare few struck their targets, but most went glancing off the walls and rattled to the floor.

This team was just plain *bad*. Despair was beginning to gnaw at the pit of John's stomach, like a bad case of indigestion. Kritta was outstanding, of course, but Kaal was so distracted, he could barely remember which was the right end of his SonicArrows, Monix threw them with sheer brute force and no precision at all, and poor Dyfi had to use both hands to even pick them up. When she threw them, they travelled about three metres, making a pitiful squeak like the air being let out of a balloon.

Tarope, though, was learning. He was nowhere near as bad as the others, and with Kritta patiently helping him, he was even getting to be pretty good. More of his arrows were hitting than missing, and the ones that weren't thrown right sounded more like mewing kittens than screeching tomcats.

"Not bad!" Kritta said, as Tarope's latest throw thudded into the Defendroid target, right in the middle of its chest. "Let's try something a bit more advanced for your last shot, OK?"

"Fine with me!" Tarope said, hopping from one foot to the other in his excitement.

"OK. Try jumping up in the air and throwing right at the top of your jump. If your opponent's blocking, you can sometimes hit them from above."

Tarope leaped, sailing into the air on his long, froggy legs, and threw.

The SonicArrow never made a sound. One moment it was leaving his hand, the next it was juddering from the target.

Tarope did a second leap, this time punching the

air. "YES!"

"Nice one, Tarope!" John called out. *Shame he couldn't be that good with the LaserPros*, he thought. *He's really cheered up now.*

Next, Kritta moved Kaal. "Time for your last shot," she told him. "Just relax. You're bound to hit the target sooner or later."

But Kaal didn't look relaxed. He glanced at Tarope, who was still celebrating, and a determined look came over his face.

He crouched down, holding his SonicArrow tight, then leaped up into the air like Tarope had. He threw the SonicArrow with a wild yell.

Obviously, in Kaal's imagination, the SonicArrow was somehow meant to fly miraculously straight and wham into the target's head, scoring maximum points and impressing Kritta.

In reality, however, John could only watch in horror, as the arrow screeched up through the air, whanged off the ceiling, flipped over, and fell point-downward into Kritta's foot. The screech that came out of her mouth was louder than the sound from any of the SonicArrows.

"Oh no!" Kaal stammered. "I'm sorry! I'm so sorry, I didn't mean for that to happen ..."

"You IDIOT!" she howled, clutching her foot and hopping up and down. "You big, clumsy, Derrilian oaf!"

"I was just trying to do a jump shot like Tarope. I thought you'd be pleased!"

"Erm," John said, as he saw the door slide open. "Guys ..."

An Examiner hovered into the sports hall and made straight for Kaal.

"KAAL TARTARU, YOU HAVE ENDANGERED A FELLOW STUDENT WITH A WEAPON. VIOLATION OF RULE EIGHT-TWO-SEVEN. PUNISHMENT IS DETENTION." It swivelled on the spot and hovered back out again.

John had to wonder how the Examiner had found out so quickly. Were the robots watching every single room from some mysterious central security station?

A second white robot came scooting into the room, but this wasn't an Examiner. John recognized the fireball insignia on its chest. It was one of the Meteor Medics, the trauma team of Hyperspace High.

The Meteor Medic scanned Kritta, and then said

gravely, "She needs immediate treatment. I'm taking her up to the medical wing."

"Shouldn't one of us go with her?" said Kaal.

"Absolutely not," the medic said coldly. It lifted Kritta gently in stretcher made of a manipulator beam, then backed out of the room, taking her with it.

"This seems like a good time to take a break," John said wearily. "Get some lunch, everyone. We'll meet back here in an hour."

After Kritta's injury and the failed SonicArrow attempts, John's team was more than ready to stop.

Alone in the empty hall, John wandered down to where the targets stood. They had recorded the number of times they'd been hit and by which student. Kritta and Tarope had scored over twenty each, but Monix had eight, John five, and Dyfi and Kaal had no hits at all.

It was too much. He spread his arms wide and yelled at the top of his voice, "Aaaaaargh! The Space Spectacular is TOMORROW! AND THIS TEAM IS A TOTAL WASHOUT! WHAT ON EARTH AM I GOING TO DO?"

CHAPTER 8

Leaving the Sonic Sports Hall, John set off towards the Centre, then paused and turned back in the other direction. It was no good; he couldn't face spending even more time with his useless team. What he needed right now was to be on his own.

Angrily, he strode towards the dorm he shared with Kaal. *Why is he so obsessed with Kritta, and being such a daft great berk*? he thought. *Doesn't he know a lost cause when he sees one*? Was it really only two days ago that Kaal had been so determined to impress his parents, and not this insect-like girl? There had to be some way to snap Kaal out of this.

Maybe having his family around tomorrow would

help. But that just made John think of the Space Spectacular, and the fact the team was still hopeless. Tarope couldn't hold a LaserPro, and Dyfi could barely even lift a SonicArrow. What was he meant to do with a team like that?

John reached his dorm and threw himself his bed. "Zepp, I've got a challenge for you."

"Go on," Zepp said.

"Can you make it sound like it's raining? It never rains in space; I miss it."

The soft patter of raindrops filled the room. John sighed heavily, as he imagined rain running down the windows of his bedroom.

"Is that any better?" Zepp asked. "I can add thunder if you wish."

"No, thanks. Just the rain is fine."

John lay on his bed and stared at the ceiling, letting the imaginary rain wash the frustration out of his head. He let out a deep sigh.

"Is that loud exhalation a human expression of frustration?" Zepp asked, perceptive as ever.

"Too right," said John. "It's just not fair. I'm stuck with being the leader, trying to pull this useless

Galactic Battle team into shape. And even if by some miracle I manage to, my parents won't even be here to see it! So what's the point, eh? What's the flipping point? Why bother?"

"Why bother?" echoed Zepp. "Because when you *do* pull it off, you'll remember it for the rest of your life, that's why!"

"Don't even joke," John said. "Why on Earth did they make me leader?"

"Because they honestly believed you could do the job," Zepp said seriously. "And you can. You're a natural leader. You've got all the traits and abilities that a good leader needs."

"Then how come I'm not getting anywhere?" John asked.

"You've been given a tough job," said Zepp. "If everything a leader had to do was easy, how would they ever find out what they were really capable of?"

"It's too tough," said John.

"But not impossible," Zepp pointed out.

"We're all so different," said John. "Tarope can't hold a LaserPro, and I can't throw a SonicArrow straight ..."

"Hmmmm," said Zepp. "Those are good observations, John. But maybe you should focus on your team's strengths instead of its weaknesses."

"Well, Monix and Kaal were pretty handy with the LaserPros, and Kritta was awesome with the SonicArrows." John quickly started feeling a bit more positive.

"Now you're starting to sound like a leader," said Zepp.

John started thinking about famous leaders from Earth he'd learned about at his old school. Some of the greatest heroes had won victories despite being the underdog. Zepp was right: good leaders didn't give up on their team.

John's mind started running through famous historic battles. The ancient Greeks beating the better-armed Persians ... Wellington crushing Napoleon's army at the Battle of Waterloo ... the outnumbered Union Army defeating the Confederates at the Battle of Gettysburg ... *What I need is a strategy that plays to the team's individual strengths*, John suddenly realized.

"So you really think I can turn this team around?"

he asked Zepp.

"Affirmative," Zepp said, without a second's hesitation. "But you have to truly believe it. Because your team won't believe in you unless you believe in yourself first."

"Wow," John said. "Thanks, Zepp. I feel a lot better now."

It was amazing what a few well-chosen words could do. Perhaps what his own team needed was a pep talk, just like Zepp had given him. He began to go over what he'd say to them.

Just as he was about to head back out, he noticed a box on his bedside table. He peered in and saw that it was full of hairy, blackish-blue objects. They looked – and smelled – like rotting pistachios.

"Neptune nuts," he read aloud from the side of the packet. "Yeuch. How did they get there?"

He turned the packet around, remembering the one and only time he'd ever tried them. They had filled his mouth with horrible, salty foam, like chewing bath bombs. *Kaal must have left them here*, he decided, and went back to join his team.

Whistling happily on his way to the Sonic Sports

Hall, John called up Ton-3 from the team sheet to see which weapon they'd be practising with that afternoon.

"Hot Shots!" the hologram announced, swaggering through the air in a long, black, trenchcoat-like garment and twirling a pistol on her finger. "These triple-barrelled pistols are the hottest weapon around! One easily replaced thermal clip loads you up with eighteen heat pellets – enough for six scorching, metal-melting triple shots! And if you need supreme firepower in a hurry, just flick the switch all the way to rapid fire!"

"Awesome," John said. "The team's going to love these."

Then Ton-3 began to gabble in a much quieter voice. "Always ensure that the safety setting on your Hot Shot is properly activated, as the manufacturer accepts no responsibility for improper use. Hot Shot is for use only in approved combat and sporting environments. Do not attempt to eat heat pellets. Do not use Hot Shot to clear blocked sinks—"

John looked down at the team sheet and found the mute button. Ton-3 was still chattering, but now silently. "Yeah, yeah, I get the picture," he said.

Dyfi met him in the doorway, brandishing a Hot Shot. "John, look! A weapon I can actually hold!"

"These are even better than the LaserPros," Tarope was saying.

Even Monix looked excited.

They were helping themselves to Hot Shot guns and fistfuls of thermal clips from an open silver box that stood against the wall. But Kaal and Kritta were nowhere to be seen.

"I guess Kaal's not out of detention yet?" John asked.

"And Kritta's still in the medical wing," Dyfi said sadly. "I hope she gets out in time for Cyber-Karaoke night. It's meant to be a blast."

Once again, the sports hall had been set up especially for them. The walls had shifted, forming a huge dome. Hovering in the air in the centre of the room was a group of star-shaped targets, outlined with red, blue, and green light. The red ones were about the size of John's head; the green ones the size of his whole body. He guessed they had different point values, based on how difficult they were to hit.

He depressed the mute button, and Ton-3 was audible again. "Ready to get started?" she asked. "OK! You need to stand in a circle and fire at the targets in the middle of the room. The smaller the target, the more points you score."

Knew it, John thought.

"Are you sure?" Monix said, sounding alarmed. "If we miss the target, we might hit the person standing on the opposite side of the room!"

"Don't you worry about that!" said Ton-3. "We've thought of that, trust me."

"OK, has everyone got plenty of ammunition?" John asked.

"Locked and loaded!" Dyfi trilled.

"Cool! Before we start, I just wanted to say a few things." He took a deep breath before continuing. "We are going to *rock* this Space Spectacular. Sure, we've had a rough start, but I bet there are other teams out there who wish they could change places with us! And we're getting better every time we practise. Monix kicks butt with a LaserPro now, and Tarope's doing better with SonicArrows than even he expected! Right?"

"Right!" yelled Tarope, giving John a thumbs-up.

"So, let's fire it up, team! Get to your places, and when you hear the signal, start blowing away those targets!"

"*Wooooh!*' yelled Dyfi and Tarope, sprinting across the room. Even Monix looked keen, as she lined up her first shot.

Now we're starting to look like a team, thought John.

The signal went off, sounding a blare like a triumphant war horn.

"Open fire!" John ordered.

Suddenly, the room lit up as if a box of fireworks had been accidentally set ablaze. The Hot Shots fired streaming, comet-like fireballs that exploded in showers of sparks when they struck a target. Waves of heat rippled in the air.

John gripped his weapon firmly, aimed for one of the high-scoring red stars, and fired. It erupted with crimson light, flashed 100 PTS, and reset itself.

I hit it! came the stunned realization. *Dead on!*

Encouraged by his success, he aimed and fired at a few more. Two hits and one near-miss! It was a lot like playing laser tag back home on Earth, running around with his friends in a dark arena, taking potshots at one another.

Dyfi was racking up hundreds of points, too. Now that she finally had a weapon she could hold properly, she was making up for lost time with a vengeance. John watched her slam heat pellets into target after target, without missing once.

"Aargh!" yelled Monix. "Can't we go back to using the LaserPros? I can't hit a thing with this stupid gun!" And as if to prove it, she let off a volley of shots that flew wide, missing the target and heading towards Dyfi.

Just as it seemed Dyfi would be obliterated, the target swivelled round and sucked the stray shots up into itself, using some sort of gravity field.

"Phew," John said with relief. "Ton-3 was right. They *did* think of that."

Tarope was doing badly, too. He'd only scored a few points and was getting frustrated, like he had with the LaserPros. "These targets are too small! How are we supposed to hit them?"

"OK, you two," John said to Tarope and Monix.

"Let's go over the basics again. The important thing is to take your time. Breathe steadily, sight down the barrel, and ..." He stopped.

Something smelled of burning. It was like when his dad left the bacon on while he was doing the crossword in the paper.

"Can you smell that?" he asked Monix.

"Yes! Something's on fire ... Oh no! TAROPE!"

"What?" Tarope said. "What's wrong?"

John stared, horrified, as little orange drops like runny candle wax fell from Tarope's arm. "Your skin's melting!"

"*Aaaargh!* Help!" Tarope squealed, dropping his Hot Shot and running around in a circle. "I need cooling before my whole skin peels off!"

"Zepp, send Meteor Medics to the Sonic Sports Hall. It's urgent!" called John.

In no time, two Meteor Medics charged into the room. Tarope was quickly scanned, lifted a force-field stretcher, and rushed to the door. One of the medics paused for a moment.

"Should I reserve hospital beds for the rest of you?" it asked darkly. "Two casualties in two days. I sense a dangerous pattern emerging."

"Will Tarope be OK?" asked Dyfi anxiously.

"Tarope is a Mucosian," the medic explained. "Extreme heat can trigger their skin-shedding cycle too early. They don't feel it, so it's more the shock than anything else. He'll be fine once we've dunked him in some chill-gel. But explain: how did he get exposed to extreme heat in the first place?"

"I know why," Monix said, holding up Tarope's Hot Shot. "The safety on his weapon wasn't on."

"Ton-3 should have told us—" started Dyfi.

"No," John said hollowly. "I should have checked them. I'm the leader. It's my fault."

Dark thoughts swirled in John's mind, as he watched Tarope being taken away. *I let my team down again.*

CHAPTER 9

"Thank you, everyone!" said Ms Vartexia, her huge blue head gleaming in the spotlight. "That was Loviata Quarmeen from year three, giving us her unforgettable rendition of last year's smash hit, 'Warpgate to My Heart'. Show your appreciation!"

The students gathered in the Centre all applauded. Loviata, who seemed to be made entirely from shifting shadows, took a bow and left the stage. Kaal had once told John in fearful tones that she only became visible in her sleep, and nobody who had seen her true shape would ever forget it again.

John had barely noticed the singing; he was too

wrapped up in his own thoughts. If he were honest, he wasn't really in the mood for this, but he hadn't wanted to walk out on the team – the team he somehow had to pull together by tomorrow. The team that could not afford to get any more detentions. He thought of the parents arriving by the hundreds, and the palms of his hands began to feel sweaty.

"That was brilliant!" Dyfi said. "I can't believe I've never been to one of these before!"

"I love Cyber-Karaoke nights," said Kritta, obviously enjoying herself, despite her bandaged foot. "They really bring the school together, don't you think?"

"I wish," John said ruefully. Although the Galactic Battle team was all together again, gathered at the Centre along with everyone else for an evening of robot-assisted karaoke, he still hadn't seen Emmie anywhere.

Kritta looked concerned. "Still worried about Emmie?"

"Yeah." John hated knowing that something was wrong, but not knowing how to fix it. "She's convinced Kaal and I did something to upset her, something dangerous. She won't talk to either of us. And now she doesn't turn up to a Cyber-Karaoke event? It's just not like her."

Kaal agreed. "It's not a proper Cyber-Karaoke night until Emmie gets up and sings. I haven't heard her sing 'Phosphene Girl' for ages. I raced over here from detention so I wouldn't miss it."

"OK! Next up is Lishtig ar Steero!" announced Ms Vartexia.

Lishtig came bounding up to the stage, his huge mass of purple hair trailing behind him. He grabbed the microphone as if it were a LaserPro. "Cue up 'Decimator' by Neutron Decay," he instructed. "Playtime's over. It's time to get *heavy*!"

Kaal quickly passed around a bag of chewy proton pieces.

"No, thanks," Dyfi said. "I don't like the taste."

"Oh, they're not for eating," Kaal said. "They're to stick in your ears."

Dyfi looked confused. "Why would anyone want to—"

At that moment, a howl of feedback ripped through the room that made SonicArrows seem like whimpering puppies by comparison.

"Oh no," Tarope said, and put his head between his knees as if he were bracing himself for a crash. "Here we go. Don't say we didn't warn you."

Lishtig flung back his shock of hair and made frenzied air-guitar motions. "Yeeeeeeaaaaahhhhhhh!" he yelled. "One, two, three, FOUR ..."

"Quick, give me some proton pieces before he starts singing," Dyfi said. She got them in her ears just in time.

"I'M A SPACE-FUELLED DECIMATOR AND GALACTIC TERMINATOR. SO DON'T ROCK THIS PLANET DEVASTATOR OR I'LL BE AN ETERNAL DOMINATOR!" roared Lishtig. The sounds blasting out of the Cyber-Karaoke speakers were like hurricane winds blowing through a dustbin factory. All around the Centre, students covered their ears and made agonized expressions.

"I think I've gone deaf!" Kritta shouted over the noise.

Lishtig whipped his hair around, belting out the lyrics: "AS MIND ERASER AND LASER BLAZER, THIS COSMIC MASTER WILL BE YOUR PLASMA BLASTER ..."

There was nothing for it but to wait for the horrendous noise to end. It was uncannily like being trapped in the Defendroid containment cell. Eventually – in a thunderous, hair-thrashing crescendo – the song finished, leaving Lishtig standing alone on stage in the spotlight with his fist raised.

The students looked on in total silence, too stunned to clap. John and his team extracted the squidgy sweets from their ears.

"Thank you very much," Lishtig's words echoed through the silent Centre. "Check out my band, Max Destructo and the Sonic Death Armada, live in concert in the engineering bay next week. Peace out!"

Looking slightly dazed, Ms Vartexia returned to the stage. "Well, I think we can all agree that was … different. Next up is Dol!"

As the dolphin-like P'Sidion girl took the microphone, Kritta gave John a nudge. "You should have a go, too."

"I don't think they've got any Earth music," he said. "I suppose I could ask, though."

The more he thought about it, the more he liked the idea. Maybe some Earth music would make him feel better – and maybe embarrassing himself on stage was a small price to pay for a taste of home.

Dol blew some bubbles in her fishbowl-like helmet, which John suspected was her way of clearing her throat. "This song is called 'Tik Tiki-kikkik, Ta Tikik Skeee Tik'," she said. "And if you know the chorus, join in! Don't be shy!"

Strange slooshing, booming sounds gushed from the speakers, as if the microphone had been lowered into a washing machine.

Dol began to squeak and click, her eyes closed with emotion. John saw that Kritta had joined in, swaying gently from side to side and making clicking noises of her own.

Everyone seemed to be enjoying it, except John. He didn't even have a clue what the song was about.

That settled it. *I need to hear something I like,* he decided. *I've had more than enough of all this weird alien music! There has to be a song I can sing. Something that reminds me of home, that really puts its finger on how I'm feeling right now …*

He thought back to his dad's CD collection and the songs they'd sung along to in the car. And he realized he knew the perfect song. It was staring him in the face.

The next few moments passed in a blur. He seemed to go from sitting with his team to talking to Ms Vartexia to being up on stage in no time at all. The next thing he knew, he was standing in a dazzling spotlight with the microphone in his hand.

The piano chords began, almost unbearably sweet and familiar, and suddenly he was singing the opening lyrics to "Rocket Man" by Elton John.

It sounded so strange and simple after all that electronic, unearthly music, but to John it was like waking from a dream and finding himself back home. He closed his eyes – he knew the words by heart, anyway – and saw the familiar sights of home so clearly: his street, his house, his own room.

He could hear the excited voices of students around him: "This is new" … "never heard him sing before" … "what kind of an instrument makes a noise like *that*" … "so this is what Earth music is like!"

The chorus was coming up. He threw himself into it, heart and soul. The lyrics, about an astronaut in space missing his family back on Earth, were bittersweet. He could never have known, back on his home planet, how fitting the words would turn out to be one day. His parents thought he was at boarding school in Derbyshire. They couldn't have guessed that he was light ears away, feeling homesick at his school in space.

Were the students enjoying the song? He couldn't tell. He kept his eyes shut until he'd finished. It made it so much easier.

When the final notes faded away, he opened his eyes, not sure what to expect.

Applause broke out all across the Centre. A few of the students gave him an odd look as he made his way back to his seat, but it was obvious that most of the students loved it, even if it was very different to what they were used to.

Kaal clapped him on the back. "That was brilliant! I love Earth music. It's all so different."

Kritta was gazing at John adoringly. "I think that was the most beautiful thing I've ever heard. You're amazing."

John had felt like he was floating on a cloud, but with that comment, he abruptly fell off it. "Maybe you should have a go next, Kaal," John suggested, hoping Kaal understood what he was really saying.

"I couldn't," Kaal mumbled. "Not with everybody watching."

"Just imagine your family's out there cheering you on!" John said. "They'll be here tomorrow."

Kaal grinned at that. "I can't wait."

"My folks are coming, too," Tarope added. "Uncle Scront is flying them here in his clapped-out old star-skiff. All fourteen of them! If it doesn't break down on the way, that is."

"My parents are on a galactic cruise," Monix said miserably.

"So they're not coming?" Dyfi asked. "That's a shame."

"No, they *are* coming! That's the problem! They've paid a fortune for the captain to divert the cruise ship to Hyperspace High for the day, just so they can be here! How embarrassing is that?"

With all this talk of visiting families, John's good mood was beginning to fade away again. Then he saw a sight that instantly cheered him up: Emmie, walking in through the Centre doors! OK, so Mordant Talliver was right behind her, but John was willing to put up with that.

There were so many questions that needed to be answered – and now it looked like there were some new ones. Why were there streaks of black in her silvery hair? And why did she look even angrier than the last time he'd seen her?

He stood up and waved. "Hey, Emmie! Over here!"

She locked eyes with John and came striding over to his table. The last time she'd been tearful, but now she looked angry enough to punch a hole through the ship's hull. "Go on," she snapped. "Have a good laugh."

John looked at her hair, at the thick, greasy-looking black stripes. "That's, uh, a new look for you. Is it for the show?"

Emmie's eyes narrowed to slits of pure fury. She glanced back at Mordant, who shook his head in a way that said, *Can you believe this guy?* She leaned in close and spoke slowly and clearly:

"This is the last warning you're going to get, John Riley. One more stunt, one more *little joke* and I'll have to tell the Examiners what you've been doing.

Got it?" Then the mask of fury cracked for a second, and she looked like she was about to cry. "I ... what did I ever do to you? To either of you?"

Mordant patted her on the shoulder, comfortingly. "Nice one, human," he said to John, his voice oozing sarcasm. "You had everyone believing you were such a good guy. Looks like you fooled them all."

With that, he steered Emmie away and walked with her to the back of the Centre. John looked at Kaal, who was sitting open-mouthed.

"What just happened?" John said, feeling like Emmie had picked him up and shaken him like a snowglobe. "Kaal, did that make any sense to you?"

Kaal pointed a talon. "John. Look."

Mordant and Emmie had sat down next to each other. Emmie leaned in to whisper something to Mordant.

Mordant laughed, leaned back in his chair, and put his arm casually around Emmie's shoulders.

"Kaal, tell me I'm not seeing this," John said hollowly.

"It can't be," Kaal echoed. "It just can't."

Emmie leaned against Mordant again, whispering

cosily in his ear. One of his tentacles draped itself across her knee.

Monix looked puzzled. "What's wrong? Do you know that couple?"

Couple, John thought, his mind squirming in horror. *Are Emmie and Mordant a couple?*

CHAPTER 10

John looked down from the edge of the pit, too scared to move. Emmie was down there, sunk up to her waist in gleaming black oil, sheer terror on her face. It wasn't just in her hair now. It was plastered over her whole body.

With both arms, she reached up to him. "Help me! Please! I can't climb out, it's too slippery ..."

John lay flat on his stomach and reached down as far as he could. His fingertips were almost brushing hers, but Emmie's hand hovered just out of reach.

"Hurry!" she begged. "He's down here with me, he's got hold of me; *he's going to pull me under!*"

Bubbles burst in the black oil. From somewhere below came the sound of thick, treacly laughter. Then two dripping black tentacles reared up from the oil and twined themselves around Emmie's arms, her neck, and her face, dragging her backward and out of John's grip. Mordant's tentacles.

Emmie let out a muffled scream, as Mordant dragged her down.

"You can't save her, John Riley," Mordant gloated, sinking down below the surface and taking Emmie with him. "She's mine now. All mine!"

"No!" John yelled.

John lunged forward, felt the edge of the pit give way, lost his balance, tumbled down into the oily depths ...

... and woke up in the dark dorm room, gasping.

The bed sheets were tangled around his legs. He was covered in sweat.

The time on the bedside clock flashed 1.03.

John groaned and sat up, rubbing his eyes. "One in the morning?" he whispered to himself, not wanting to believe it.

Even though the screen to Kaal's bed pod was shut,

John could hear his room-mate tossing and turning. It didn't sound like his best friend was sleeping well, either. Kaal, being a Derrilian, only needed one hour's sleep a night – but it looked like even *that* was troubled.

John went to the bathroom to get a drink of water. The sudden glare when he switched on the light was dazzling. His reflection, tousle-haired and puffy-faced, looked rough.

"That was pretty crazy," he told himself hoarsely.

John didn't need to be a genius to work out what that nightmare was about. Mordant, Emmie, and the Space Spectacular ... they were all preying on his mind.

"Hey, John," Zepp said in a hushed voice. "Are you OK? I was monitoring your brainwaves just then, and there was a LOT going on in that head of yours."

"Had a nightmare," John said. "Zepp ... what time is it on Earth? At my parents' house, I mean."

"Eight fifteen in the morning," Zepp said. "Want me to put a call through?"

"I'd love that!"

John sat down in front of his vidphone in his bed

pod, just in case his parents accidentally caught a glimpse of Kaal. The computer sounded its dialling noises, and almost instantly, his mum and dad were there on the screen.

"John!" his mum exclaimed. "You're still in pyjamas! Shouldn't you be dressed?"

"It's a boarding school," his dad put in. "They run them like holiday camps nowadays. None of that up-at-six-for-a-cross-country-run stuff!" And he gave John a wink. "Good to see you, John. How's school life?"

"It's crazy," John said. "How are you? How's Super Rover?"

"The dog," his father said levelly, "is certifiably insane. But he's a Jack Russell, so that's perfectly normal. He runs around the house, shows no respect for other people's property, eats like every meal is his last, and sleeps whenever he feels like it. Now I think about it, it's just like having you back home."

John laughed. "I've missed you too, Dad."

It hurt his heart to be so far away from his parents, and it was a bittersweet feeling to talk to them now. *But,* he thought, *that's the price I have to pay for going to school on an awesome spaceship. And there's not a boy on Earth who wouldn't want to change places with me.*

He spent the next ten minutes speaking with his parents about everything from town gossip to the football league tables. Mostly he had to duck the questions about his school friends, but he couldn't just say *nothing*, so he'd come up with a trick weeks ago to keep them from suspecting anything was going on. By changing the names a bit, he could tell them a few things – so Kaal became his best friend "Carl", Emmie became "Emma", and Mordant became "nasty Morton". It helped get things off his chest ... a little.

"I should go," he said eventually. "I'm in a school show with Carl, and today's the dress rehearsal."

"A show?" his mother exclaimed. "Like when you did *Oliver*? That's brilliant! We'll come and see you, of course."

John struggled to come up with an excuse on the spot. "It's in the morning when you'd be at work," he fibbed.

His dad shrugged. "That's no problem. We'll just take some time off."

"No, really, don't go to the trouble," John said desperately. "It's not really a show, it's more of … um … a demonstration. Stuff we've learned. Very boring." He winced inwardly as he said it. *I wish you COULD be here*, he thought.

A rather hasty goodbye later, he switched off the ThinScreen and clambered back into bed.

He was asleep in less than a minute. This time, he did not dream.

The alarm went off at eight o'clock. John struggled out of bed, feeling only half alive. Kaal came out of the shower, looking bleary and haggard.

"You look like I feel," John said. "And I feel terrible."

"I've made such an idiot of myself," Kaal said. "I've ruined everything. I should have known the Wakan-Dothak would never work with Kritta. And I wasn't brave enough to do karaoke to impress her. I've tried to think of other ways to get her to like me, but I can't think of a single one."

"We'd better get ready to face the world," John said reluctantly.

"Can't we just hide in the dorm all day?" Kaal said.

"We could pretend to be ill. I *feel* ill."

But there was no avoiding it. With many a moan and groan, John and Kaal got dressed and braced themselves to leave their room.

"Here we go," John said, heading out into the corridor.

To his amazement, Hyperspace High was already swarming with unearthly beings – even more so than usual. Through the corridor windows, he could see a huge convoy of spaceships steadily arriving at the docking bay, from a discoloured old shoebox-like vessel held together with metal plates to a vast rotating saucer-ship glimmering with thousands of lights. The families had clearly started arriving long before the Space Spectacular was due to begin.

"That's Emmie's family!" said Kaal, pointing to the saucer. "Amazing ship they've got!"

John had never seen so many different ships in one place. Emmie's family's ship was a sparkling golden colour, a huge saucer encircled by silver and gold laser beams. It seemed to pulse and glow with energy. Some of the stranger ships also caught John's eye – a trident-like white cruiser with a glowing ball at the rear, a manta ray-like craft with graceful outlines and transparent fin sections, a dark V-wing with sinister red lights tracking back and forth, and a dumpy spaceship shaped like a bowler hat that John was sure he'd seen in an old book about UFOs.

Kaal joined him at the window and gave a yell of excitement. "I can see my dad's ship! Look, John!"

The Derrilian cruiser was almost at the head of the line. It was a rugged, gunmetal ship with transparent orange-red wings spread out on either side.

"Energy collectors," Kaal explained. As they watched, the wings folded themselves smoothly away and the ship moved in to dock.

"Come on!" Kaal yelled, running off down the corridor. "Come and meet my family!"

"Just try and stop me," John said, running after him. Both of them suddenly forgot how tired they had been moments before.

As they waited in the reception rooms by the hangar bay, Kaal fidgeted in excitement. Some of the students who'd witnessed the Wakan-Dothak laughed, whispering to one another and making flapping motions with their hands, but Kaal – for once

– didn't seem to care a bit. The doors finally slid open, allowing the latest group of visiting families to flood into the school.

"There they are!" Kaal cried out. "Look! Can you see them?"

"Yeah!" John said, laughing. Kaal's whole family loomed head and shoulders above all the other families, so they weren't exactly hard to spot. They were wearing long garments that reminded John of Roman togas. Kaal's mother had a silver headband with ornamental horns on it, while his sister Kulvi had a wrap-around white visor over her eyes. John wondered if it was a high-tech pair of sunglasses.

With much waving across the room, followed shortly after by much joyous flapping of wings, Kaal and his family were reunited. John solemnly wished them all "wide skies".

Mr Tartaru clasped John's hand in his own scaly talons and shook it vigorously, saying, "Kaal tells me this is how you say hello on Earth."

Then Kaal's sister Kulvi lunged over to bite him on the face.

John yelped and backed away.

Kulvi grinned. "Gotcha! Kaal told me he got you once with the old face-biting gag, but I didn't expect it to work twice!"

John rolled his eyes. "Very funny."

"Don't tease John too much, Kulvi," said Mr Tartaru firmly. "He's an honorary member of our family for today, don't forget. And the journey's over now, so take that 3-D movie viewer off!"

"I am?" John boggled. Kulvi grumpily folded away the visor.

"Of course you are!" boomed Mr Tartaru. "Since your own family cannot be here, I would like to consider you as part of mine. It is the Derrilian way: no hatchling left behind! If you have no objection, of course."

"Are you kidding? I'd love that!"

"Welcome to the family, brother," beamed Kaal. "But where's Varka, Dad?"

"Grandfather Kresh is looking after her," said Mr Tartaru. "Sorry to disappoint you, son, but she's still too little for a long journey, especially just after her first moulting."

"I don't suppose either of you have had breakfast

yet?" Kaal's mother said. Seeing the looks on their faces, she added, "No, I thought not. Right, everyone. Let's eat."

"The Centre's going to be heaving right now!" said John worriedly, looking around. "All these families – we won't get a place!"

"I already booked us a table before we even docked here," said Kaal's mother, brandishing a ThinScreen. "Honestly, I don't know what you'd all do without me around."

As they took a TravelTube to the Centre, John's thoughts strayed back to the Space Spectacular. It was *this evening*. His stomach knotted. No matter how he turned it around in his head, he couldn't see how he was supposed to make Tarope any less hopeless with a LaserPro, or teach Dyfi how to throw a SonicArrow, or show Monix how to hit a target with a Hot Shot. Training them all properly would take ages, and there just wasn't time – not to mention the fact that he wasn't exactly an expert in them himself.

Once again, he wished he'd never been chosen as team leader. It wasn't fun being the person in charge of doing the impossible.

"So!" said Kaal's dad, as they sat down to breakfast. "Kaal tells me you're his team leader!"

Great timing, John thought. "That's right, Mr Tartaru."

"Please. You must call me Vorn. And Kaal's mother is Dulâna."

The food – most of it looking like multicoloured seaweed – came humming up through holes that opened in the table, and all the Derrilians tucked in. Luckily, Zepp provided John with a bowl of cornflakes.

"So who's the leader of your planet, John?" Kaal's mother asked.

"M-u-u-um," said Kaal. "Don't pester him."

"I'm not pestering at all, I'm simply curious. I'm sure John doesn't mind; do you, dear? Now, do you have a robotic overseer, or do you use global telepathy to select your planetary leader?"

"We don't actually have one leader for the whole planet," John explained. "All the different countries have their own leader."

Kaal's mother almost choked on her food. "How … what … really? Every country for itself?"

"Pretty much."

"That's madness! Anarchy! No wonder you haven't developed interstellar travel yet!"

"Now you've done it," Kulvi said. "She'll offer to come and run your planet for you, just you wait."

"Now then, Dulâna," said Kaal's dad. "Different worlds have different cultures, and we have to respect them – even if they seem strange to us."

"I just feel sorry for the poor things!" Kaal's mother protested.

"Well, I think Earth sounds brilliant," Kulvi said. "Shame we can't go there for a holiday. Some of their life forms look delicious."

Once breakfast had been chomped, slurped, and noisily chewed, John and Kaal stood up.

"We need to meet up with the rest of the team," John explained. "Dress rehearsal's in ten minutes."

"Good luck, boys," said Kaal's father. "We'll see you on stage later!"

An idea was bubbling up in John's mind. Kaal's family were all very different, but they all had something special to offer. Vorn was firm and fair, Dulâna was hyper-organized and efficient, Kulvi was funny ... and nobody tried to be everything at once. In a way, they reminded him of his team. Maybe this was the answer he'd been looking for ...

There was just enough time to change into their special lightspeed suits – flashier, silver versions of their battle suits, with neon yellow triangles on the chest – before meeting the others in the Junkyard to collect their weapons. Everyone had been supplied with a bright yellow belt, a clip for a LaserPro, and containers for thermal pellets, plus a back-slung quiver to hold plenty of SonicArrows.

Kritta's injured foot was freshly healed (the Meteor Medics and their nano-surgeons had seen to that), and Tarope's skin was all where it was supposed to be, with none of it melting off. Nonetheless, the team met his gaze with anxious eyes. They were obviously as worried as he had been.

"Should we all get these belts and quivers on?" Kritta asked.

"Hold on a sec first," John said. "There's been a change of plan. From now on, everyone's going to stick to the weapon they're best with."

"But didn't Ton-3 say we had to use all three?" Dyfi asked.

"The *team* has to use all three," John explained. "But it doesn't say we *each* have to. So, Monix, you and Kaal are on LaserPros. Dyfi, you and me will take the Hot Shots. Tarope and Kritta, you can work your magic with the SonicArrows. That sound good to everyone?"

"It sounds better than good!" Tarope said. "Getting us all to play to our strengths – it's so obvious!"

"Why didn't we think of that?" sighed Kritta.

"Maybe we just needed someone to point out the obvious," Monix said with a crooked smile. John thought she sounded almost proud of him.

"So, what are we waiting for?" he yelled. "Let's tool up, and get ready to kick some Defendroid butt!"

CHAPTER 11

John took the lead, as the team picked up their weapons and charged excitedly out of the Technology classroom and down the hallway. A little squirrel-like alien covered in rubbery spikes squeaked and dived for cover as they approached, wielding their LaserPros, Hot Shots, and SonicArrows. Crowds up ahead parted to let them through.

I hope none of the parents think the ship's under attack, John thought, as they sprinted past.

The team came to a bridge spanning the botanical sector. Huge green growths and twitching extraterrestrial plants lay beneath, safe within hydroponic enclosures. John could hear the other team members stampeding behind him.

Then he saw it – the white form of an Examiner, moving towards him from the other end of the bridge. John and the others came to a sudden scrambling halt in the middle.

"WARNING," said the Examiner ominously. "RUNNING IN THE CORRIDORS IS PROHIBITED. NO FURTHER WARNING WILL BE ISSUED. A SECOND OFFENCE WILL RESULT IN DETENTION."

As it glided away, Kaal and John looked at one another.

"Another detention and we're out!" Kaal said. "We can't risk it!"

"OK, everyone," John said. "No more running. Just walk very fast."

As briskly as they dared, they continued to hurry along. Puzzled faces turned to look at them, but John didn't care any more.

There'll be a lot more people looking at us tonight, he thought, *and that's what's important.*

"Finally!" John said as they reached the Sonic Sports Hall. He punched in the codes and then led the team inside. "OK, let's get this set up. We're going to need star targets for the Hot Shots, dummy Defendroids for the SonicArrows, and a fenced-off sparring arena for the LaserPros."

The team set to work, arranging the equipment.

Tarope hesitated. "Since this is dress rehearsal, shouldn't we be fighting the *real* Defendroids now, like we will be on stage?"

"Good question," John said, quickly pressing the HELP icon on the team sheet.

Ton-3's holographic form popped up, once again in her cheerleader outfit of bright yellow T-shirt and shorts.

"That's not possible," she said, shaking her head. "Since the Defendroids are part of the ship's defence system, they are on standby while all your parents' ships dock with us. You're fighting the real thing tonight, but for now, they're needed for protection."

Once the room was set up, John addressed the team. "Kaal and Monix, work on your sparring together. Everyone else, it's target practice. Let's go!"

LaserPros were ignited, thermal clips were slammed into Hot Shots, SonicArrows hummed into life, and the dress rehearsal began.

John had to split his time between firing at his targets and keeping an eye on the other team members. After a straight run of nine hits out of ten, he decided it was time for a tour of the room.

Kaal and Monix were going at it like gladiators. She was fast, zooming around him and slashing, first high then low, but Kaal's reaction time was spot on. As they grew more confident, they started to use flashier moves, with Kaal leaping over Monix's blade, and then jumping over her to spin around and deliver a reverse strike.

"Since you can both fly," John called to them, "try fighting in the air. The Defendroids won't be able to follow you there, so you'll have clearer shots at them."

The air bout was clumsier, but it looked amazing. Kaal's LaserPro lit up his huge wings from within and made him look like a flaming demon. When he finally got the better of Monix and slammed his LaserPro past her guard, she fell like a meteorite and slammed into the floor.

John ran forward, praying there hadn't been another injury.

But Monix shook herself and shot back up into the air. "Don't worry, I'm fine," she said, "I just did it to look spectacular!"

On the other side of the room, Dyfi was pelting the target with blasts from her Hot Shot, a look of absolute concentration on her little face. Kritta and Tarope were flinging their SonicArrows at the targets, hitting most of them. He'd heard one or two shrieks so far, but at least they came from mis-thrown SonicArrows and not from impaled teammates. At any rate, they were doing even better than yesterday.

"Looking good," he said approvingly. "Kaal, Tarope, can you get over here for a sec? I want to try something."

"What's the plan, team leader?" Tarope said.

"Kaal, can you try throwing Tarope straight up in the air, as hard as you can? Then Tarope, you take your shot. I want this to be the most devastating jump shot ever."

"Let's do it!" Tarope said. "I love this plan!"

Kaal grabbed Tarope around the waist. "One, two, three!"

The froggy student soared through the air, almost

reaching the ceiling. Then there was a silvery flash as he threw his SonicArrow, and a solid juddering noise as it hit the target dead on.

Tarope did an acrobatic flip and landed with barely a sound.

Everyone clapped and cheered.

"Wowsers," John said, a grin encompassing his face. "I know the Defendroids are tough, but a shot like that should stop anything."

The rest of the day passed in a blur. With only a brief pause for lunch, they practised their moves and honed their skills, over and over again. The team that only days earlier had been so hopeless was now a tight, well-disciplined unit, ready to back up one another.

"You think we're ready to face the real Defendroids?" Dyfi asked, her Hot Shot still glowing. For such a tiny alien, she looked dangerous.

John nodded. "We're ready."

Suddenly, an urgent-sounding alarm rang out from the ship's tannoy system.

"The Space Spectacular is about to begin!" announced Zepp. "Students have fifteen minutes to

154

reach the Centre!"

"And not a moment too soon," John said. "Monix, Dyfi, Tarope, you guys take our weapons to the Centre and let them know we're on our way. Kaal and Kritta, come with me. We're going to the Belly to collect the Defendroids."

John, Kaal, and Kritta did their best to hurry, but every other student in the school – as well as their parents – seemed to be heading the other way. All the students were wearing their team colours now, and every leader clutched their team sheet.

Rushing through the corridor, John nearly ran smack into Mordant Talliver.

Mordant looked John up and down, and his eyes narrowed in to the old familiar look of hate. But all he said was, "The Centre's the other way, John. Better hurry."

"Thanks for that," John said coldly. Had Mordant ever called him "John" before? He usually called him by his surname – or worse, "primitive Earthling".

Mordant smiled tightly and passed him by. But there, hurrying along through the crowds a few paces behind Mordant, was Emmie, clutching a bundle of shredded silver fabric. John's heart clenched painfully in his chest.

She caught his eye and scowled, but she didn't look away.

Well, at least she's not blanking me, John assured himself.

"Emmie!" he said. "Where have you been?"

"Like you care!" she spat. "Don't come over all nice with me. I know very well what you did."

John's throat tightened. He couldn't get the words out. "Wha— what?"

Emmie's hair seemed to crackle and stand on end, like an angry cat puffing itself up. She held out the fabric, which unrolled before them. It was the remains of a lightspeed suit, clawed to tatters.

"After everything else, now you do this? I thought you were my best friends!" she shouted. "I hate you both! I never want to speak to you again!"

John couldn't remember ever seeing Emmie like this before. He'd seen her upset, but never furious. It took the wind out of him, like he'd been punched in the stomach. Fortunately, Kaal came to his rescue.

"What do you mean?" Kaal replied, sounding

deeply hurt. "Who's torn your suit to pieces?"

"I thought you were clever, Kaal," Mordant jeered. "But I see you're stupid enough to stand in front of Emmie and lie to her face. How can you, of all people, ask who tore her suit up?"

Mordant held the suit next to Kaal's broad hands. The ragged strips exactly matched the pattern of Kaal's claws.

"Like I told you," Mordant said to Emmie, "it had to be a Derrilian. Look at him. There's guilt written all over his stupid green face."

Emmie nodded. "I can understand you guys being jealous of our team. But trying to ruin our performance? That's just cruel."

John looked from Mordant's angry snarl to the miserable remains of Emmie's suit, and the pieces fell into place with an almost audible click.

That little creep has framed us. He tore that suit up himself – I'd bet my life on it. He's set all this up to poison Emmie's mind against us!

John opened his mouth to accuse Mordant, but at that very moment a warning chime rang out.

"All students make their way to the Centre

immediately! The Space Spectacular is about to commence!"

Mordant twined a black tentacle around Emmie's wrist.

"Off to the Centre with you, Emmie dear. *Now.*" And away Mordant pulled Emmie, before John had a chance to reply.

"Should we go after them?" Kaal asked.

"We can't," John said. "We have to fetch the Defendroids ... only ten minutes to go!"

"I can't understand why she's angry," Kaal said, dodging out of the way of a family of wobbling beings that looked like heaps of frogspawn. "What does she think we've done?"

"Err, just a guess, but maybe what you did to her lightspeed suit?" Kritta snapped. "Come off it, Kaal. Don't play dumb."

"But I didn't do it!" Kaal protested. "I wouldn't – she's our friend!"

"And Mordant's a liar!" John said angrily. "Kritta, Kaal's telling the truth. He'd never do something like that."

"It wouldn't be the first idiotic thing he's done,"

Kritta said.

"Kritta, please!" Kaal begged.

"And then there's the other stuff!" she continued.

John rounded on her. "What *other stuff*?"

Walking to the service lift, they saw Mordant's Serve-U-Droid, G-Vez, flying down the corridor, clearly in a rush. *Off doing his lying masters' bidding again*, John thought angrily. He couldn't imagine a fate worse than being Mordant's servant.

As they entered the lift, Kritta took a breath and started to speak: "Well ... last night I was talking to Shazilda, OK, and she's best friends with Vonique-Eight, who's on the Emmie's team, and she told *me* that Vonique-Eight told *her* that Emmie was crying at Zero-G Acrobatics practice, because someone put oil in her shampoo. And Mordant told *her* that you both did it! He said he could *prove* it."

"Mordant blasted Talliver!" John roared. "One of these days that slimy creep's going to get what's coming to him."

"There's more to this than you've told us, isn't there, Kritta?" Kaal said sternly.

Kritta nodded slowly. "I don't know what exactly,

but yeah. From what I heard, Emmie thinks you've both been horrible to her for *days*. And Mordant's been her shoulder to cry on since it all started."

"Oh, I *bet* he has! He's set this whole thing up to steal Emmie's friendship from us. I'm going to tie his tentacles around his scrawny neck!" John raged.

Just then, the lift doors opened with a low grating noise. The three students made their way through the gloomy tunnels towards the Defendroids' cell.

Something's wrong here, John thought. *What is it?*

"I never really believed *you* did it, John!" Kritta burst out, sounding on the verge of tears. "I know you wouldn't!"

"But you believed *I* did?" Kaal asked miserably. "Is that what you're saying?"

"You saw the suit," Kritta said. "Those were your claw marks! Honestly, Kaal, with the weird way you've been acting lately, I don't know what to believe!"

"Er, guys?" said John, cutting off whatever Kaal was about to say. "Is it just me, or is it kind of quiet down here?"

"Now you mention it, yeah," said Kaal. "It was a lot louder last time we came down!"

John turned the corner, feeling rising dread at what he might find. There, looming in front of them, was the cell with the huge window. The Defendroids were inside, just like before. But they weren't roaring and crashing about.

Instead, their great shoulders sagged and their heads hung down on their chests. Not one of them moved or made a sound.

They looked as dead as iron statues.

CHAPTER 12

"What are we going to do about the show?" cried Kritta.

"Maybe Master Tronic can help," said John. "Zepp, can you please get Master Tronic."

"Master Tronic is on the other side of the ship. He is making some last-minute adjustments to the stage," replied the ship's computer.

"Well, what about Lorem? Is he around?" John asked, trying not to sound as panicked as he felt.

"The headmaster is about to deliver his opening remarks to the parents," answered Zepp.

"Oh, great!" wailed Kritta. "My first Space

Spectacular, and my parents aren't going to get to see me perform. The Galactic Battle team is ruined, thanks to these hunks of junk!"

"We are NOT ruined," said John firmly. "And we are NOT going to give up." John felt determined to find a solution.

"I've got my pocket ToTool with me. I could try to get them working again,' Kaal offered.

"Are you crazy?" shrieked Kritta. "Those things are dangerous and we aren't armed!"

"Don't worry," Kaal said bravely. "I'll be absolutely fine if they're in training mode."

John hesitated. The huge robots looked totally dead – but Kritta was right. It was risky. He desperately wanted to be able to do the show, but it wasn't worth endangering his best friend. Kritta and Kaal both looked at him expectantly. As team leader, it was his call.

Surely Zepp or Lorem would step in if anything went seriously wrong. John took a deep breath. "I say it's worth a shot."

Just as he was about to tap the training mode code into the panel, John stopped and stared. "Wait.

The readout says they've been put in training mode already!"

"That means someone else has been down here," Kaal said. "Someone who knew how to make the Defendroids safe to approach."

"But who else knew the code?" Kritta asked. "You don't think it was someone on our own team, do you?"

"No time to wonder about that now," said John. "Come on!" He pressed the control and the great doors groaned open.

Kaal ran to Crusher, the nearest Defendroid, a force-wrench and digital decoupler in hand. With a whizz of unfastening screws, the Defendroid's control panel swung open. Inside was a spaghetti-like mess of cables, with glassy-looking spheres and glowing junction boxes nestled among them.

"Come on," muttered Kaal. "There's got to be a central servomotor unit."

Kaal rummaged through Crusher's innards, found a thick length of what looked to John like a blue vacuum cleaner hose, and tracked back along its length to a translucent module like an Easter egg.

"Here it is. Whoa! Someone's ripped out the main

cerebral interface link."

"Translation, please?" John said.

"Essentially, their brains can't communicate with their bodies. It's sabotage. These robots have been paralysed."

"Can you fix them?" John demanded anxiously.

Kaal looked worried. "I can try to run a bypass, but it's risky. These things may look like brutes, but their circuits are delicate. If I mess it up, the feedback could fry their brains completely."

"We don't have a choice. Better get on with it."

Frowning hard in concentration, Kaal unplugged some cables, twisted them together, and plugged them in to new places, talking to himself as he worked. "OK, that's the synaptic bridge ... now the main neurolink ... I've got to fuse them ..."

There was a fizz of arcing electricity and a bright glare, as Kaal welded something loose back into place with the ToTool.

Suddenly, Crusher's eyes lit up. Its head lurched upward. It lifted its huge arm. Slowly, it turned to face John.

"READY FOR ORDERS," it grated.

"Phew," said Kaal. "I guess it worked after all! Now for the others."

John checked the time. Eight more minutes. "Come *on*, Kaal!" he muttered.

Kaal's huge fingers worked frantically, opening up robot after robot. "I'm really not sure about this, John!" he said, as one robot after another sparked into life. "I've never done this kind of repair work before."

"I can see why you were a Robot Warriors champion," Kritta said, admiration creeping into her voice.

"I wish we could just go to the Junkyard," Kaal moaned. "There's no spare parts, so I'm having to borrow bits from one section to fix another! I'm sure I've broken something, somewhere."

"You're doing great!" John reassured him.

"There," Kaal panted, stepping back. Steel Storm, the last of the Defendroids to be repaired, straightened up with an odd mechanical *buzz-click*. "I just hope that's good enough."

"It'll have to be," said John. "We haven't time to do anything else!"

The corridors were worryingly empty as the three teammates hurried to the Centre. The Defendroids pounded along behind them, their footfalls shaking the floor.

"Everyone must be inside already!" Kaal gasped. "I hope we're not too late!"

Lorem's amplified voice echoed through the empty corridors. "Welcome, one and all, to the Space Spectacular! And an especially hearty welcome to all the parents who have joined us today, from systems as far apart as Zeta Reticuli and Deneb!"

"We're missing the opening speech," Kritta moaned.

It's so hard not to break into a run! John thought. *Maybe we should risk it. There are no Examiners around, after all.*

Then he thought of how Mordant would taunt him if John spent the Space Spectacular in detention. He walked briskly, refusing to run.

The three teammates crashed through the doors of the Centre a full five minutes late. Heads nearby turned to stare at them, but most eyes were still fixed on Lorem. The Centre had been returned to its deep black amphitheatre shape, with the swollen black MorphSeats.

"Looks like we're just in time!" Kaal whispered.

Ms Vartexia came bustling over. "There you are! Right. Get down to the preparation room straight away. Down those steps. Hurry!"

The preparation area, hidden away below the Centre, was a combination of dressing room and observation lounge. An arched tunnel led up to the main stage. Screens on all the walls showed different views of the stage up above. John guessed that had to be Lorem's thoughtful doing, to ensure the students didn't miss each other's performances. Most of the gathered teams were watching Lorem's welcoming speech, but a few were going through last-minute briefings.

John, Kaal, and Kritta left the Defendroids parked against the back wall and met up with the rest of their Galactic Battle team in front of the main viewing screen. John looked around for Emmie, and caught a brief glimpse of her silver hair vanishing up the tunnel along with the rest of her team. *Just my luck that they're on first,* he thought ruefully.

Lorem, who looked even more dazzling than usual under the stage lighting, concluded his welcome speech: "So, without further ado, I am proud to present the Zero-G Acrobatics team! Zepp, if you would activate the ZeBub, please?"

The dim outline of a sphere appeared, enclosing most of the empty space at the heart of the Centre. Booming symphonic music began to play.

John watched the screen, his heart pounding. Emmie, Mordant, and a troupe of other silver-suited students walked up the steps to the stage and launched themselves into the ZeBub, tumbling in mid-air flips and coming to a stop at the top of the sphere. Arms and legs outspread, they formed an arch of star-like figures. Their team was far larger than the Galactic Battle team, John now saw; there were at least twenty of them.

I wish I could have talked to Emmie before she went out on stage, John thought. *If only we'd been quicker getting here!* In spite of everything else to contend with today, he *had* to tell her that Mordant had framed them all along.

John noticed that all of the performers in the

Zero-G Acrobatic team wore jet-belts. It seemed to be part of the equipment, since you couldn't manoeuvre in zero-gravity without some sort of propulsion, but on these belts, the jet blasts had been tinted with coloured smoke.

As the acrobatics display continued, Mordant and Emmie gently span out from the group in opposite directions, leaving rainbow trails in their wake. The rest of the group followed, half going one way and half the other.

"*Oooh!*" came the gasp from the crowd.

John watched, as amazed as the rest of the audience.

Emmie and Mordant leaped out into the centre of the ZeBub and clasped hands, rotating around one another. John strained to catch a glimpse of her face. She was smiling, but to John it looked fake – all part of the act.

Next, two more acrobats leaped in and joined them, followed by two more. The combined vapour trails made a luminous wheel effect. Eventually, the entire team was whirling like a Catherine wheel. It reminded John of something very familiar – and then he saw it. They were imitating a spiral galaxy.

John's jaw dropped. He'd never seen a student performance as stunning as this. It was like a fabulous underwater ballet crossed with a fireworks display.

"How are we going to follow this?" Kritta whispered, her insect eyes appearing even bigger than usual.

"Let's worry about that when it's our turn!" John said.

The acrobats began to break away from the galaxy formation, flying out in a starburst of colours. Eventually, only Emmie and Mordant were left, spinning faster and faster.

John held his breath. *This could be the moment!* It would be so easy for Mordant to let go of her now. And if he did, Emmie would fly straight out of the ZeBub, and over the heads of the crowd, in full gravity.

But to his relief, Mordant didn't drop her. Instead, they began to rise together, then broke away and fired their jet-belts at once, gracefully completing a full rotation and touching down on the stage feet-first.

The other acrobats steadily landed behind them, like starfighters coming back to base. The crowd applauded wildly. John joined in, primarily out of relief that Emmie was OK.

Immediately afterwards, the Traditional Music team headed up to replace the Zero-G Acrobatics team, who had begun walking back into the backstage area looking exhausted but triumphant.

Mordant smirked at John, as if to say, "Follow that!" but his expression changed to one of horror, when he caught sight of the Defendroids at the back of the room.

"What's the matter?" John yelled. "Surprised to see them working, are you?"

"How did—" Mordant started to say, then stopped himself.

Behind him, Emmie looked puzzled. "Mordant? What's wrong?"

"Stay out of this!" Mordant snapped. He beckoned over G-Vez and whispered something. John couldn't hear what Mordant was saying, but from the furious look in his yellow eyes, it was obvious that G-Vez was getting a vicious telling-off.

"I'm sorry, young master," said G-Vez, bobbing apologetically. "I followed your instructions exactly. I deactivated the Def—"

"Get lost, or I'll throw you in the Junkyard!" interrupted Mordant. Then he turned to Emmie and grabbed her arm. "Come on," he hissed. "Let's go watch the other acts."

"I've got a lot to think about right now," she shot back, yanking her arm out of Mordant's grip. "Alone!"

And with that, she ran from the room, vanishing up the back stairs.

Mordant stood, fuming, then rejoined his team and their celebrations.

What should I do now? John wondered. There was no way he could chase after Emmie – he needed to be here with his team – although he badly wanted to talk to her. Had the penny finally dropped for her? Did she realize that Mordant had used G-Vez to sabotage the Defendroids?

As John waited for his team's turn, he continued to watch the Spectacular. The Traditional Music team was still on stage, and it turned out to be a Callifraxian orchestral suite. Students drummed on opal-coloured shells and blew trombone-like notes from labyrinthine glass pipes. On any other day, it might have been soothing to listen to, but John was far too tense to enjoy it today.

He chewed his fingernails throughout the Plasma Sculpting and Star Dance displays. He barely noticed the performing Kvellian Razorbeasts, Brainsquids and Braxian Firehounds in the Alien Life Form Training act. And all through Live Holo-Theatre, he could think of nothing but his own upcoming performance.

Finally, Lorem called out, "For our last act today, it is my great pleasure to present the Galactic Battle team!"

Together, the team strode the blazing stage. The audience began to clap and then gasped as soon as they saw the immense Defendroids stomp onstage behind them.

"Please don't be alarmed," Lorem said. "Although they seem menacing, the Defendroids are perfectly safe."

The Defendroids moved to form a line at one end of the stage. John and the others formed a line at the other. He checked that his Hot Shot was fully loaded.

We can do this, he thought. *After everything we've been through, everything we've learned, I know we can defeat these things.*

John's teammates stood by his side, their weapons at the ready. They looked cool, confident, and braced to attack.

"Attack will begin in five," boomed an automated voice, "four, three ..."

"OK, guys," John whispered. "This is it. Good luck!"

"Two, one. Activate."

The Defendroids lumbered forward as one.

Kaal and Monix ignited their LaserPros and ran forward, hacking and slicing at the robots. Whizzing SonicArrows flew across the stage, striking sparks off the robots where they hit. Dyfi scored an instant headshot on Dicer, causing the oncoming robot to stagger and fall to one metal knee.

John lined up his first shot and fired. It slammed into Steel Storm's chest. The robot's eyes blazed red, and it let out a rattling roar. Currents of raw electricity writhed over its upraised fist. Then the machine ran faster towards John.

That didn't happen in practice! he thought. *They're supposed to retreat when we hit them, not fight back!*

Quickly, John looked closer at the other Defendroids. They were acting the same. The more the team hit them, the more aggressive they seemed to get.

A sudden cold flash of realization dawned. *They're in full aggression mode!* John thought.

CHAPTER 13

The Defendroids were advancing, and they weren't playing games.

"HYPERSPACE HIGH UNDER ATTACK!" they roared. "DESTROY ALL HOSTILES."

"Uh oh, guys," said Kaal. "I think my repairs might have overridden the training mode setting."

"I don't want to be destroyed!" Dyfi wailed, just as Crusher was bearing down on her, its huge feet threatening to squash her like a cockroach.

Monix slashed hard with her LaserPro, knocking one of Crusher's legs out from under it.

As Crusher tottered, Dyfi took aim with her Hot

Shot and blasted it in the chest. The robot clutched at the ground, struggling to get up.

The audience yelled encouragement, cheering and clapping.

"Go, Dyfi. Go!" squeaked a high-pitched voice from somewhere in the crowd – a voice similar to Dyfi's. It had to be someone from her family.

They think it's part of the act! thought John. *We're about to get bashed to a pulp, and they're applauding!*

Meanwhile, Kaal was in trouble. He'd run further across the stage than any of the others, and now he found himself facing Lasher, Slicer, and Steel Storm all at once. Holding his LaserPro in both hands, he frantically struck out around him, driving them back. His LaserPro was like a whirling bar of white-hot metal, striking sprays of sparks wherever it hit.

Slicer and Steel Storm fell back, but Lasher was whirling its arm faster and faster, creating a shield of spinning metal. Kaal tried to strike through it, but the Defendroid knocked Kaal's LaserPro clean out of his hands.

Lasher's wrecking-ball arm curled up like a scorpion sting, ready to strike. The audience gasped. One blow, and Kaal's flying days would be over – perhaps even his life.

"Tarope! Kritta!" John yelled. "Help Kaal!"

Tarope and Kritta quickly exchanged glances and nodded. They each threw a SonicArrow. The silvery shafts struck home in Lasher's neck, jamming themselves deep into the machinery.

The Defendroid gave a juddering roar and clutched at the embedded weapons with its claw hand, trying to tug them free.

Kaal seized the opportunity to snatch up his LaserPro, then leaped over Lasher's head and glided back down on the other side.

"That was too close!" he gasped.

The Galactic Battle team was back together now, all gathered on the side of the stage where they'd started. But the Defendroids were rallying, too. Steel Storm grabbed the fallen Crusher's upper arm, and the sudden surge of electricity seemed to revive the fallen robot. It groped its way back to its feet.

End of round one, John thought. *We're still alive – for now.*

However, the audience was loving every moment.

A fresh round of applause resounded around the Centre.

Steel Storm swivelled its enormous head to the left and right. "MULTIPLE ADDITIONAL TARGETS DETECTED!" it boomed, its voice deeper than the rest. "POTENTIALLY HOSTILE. ALL DEFENDROIDS, MOVE TO TERMINATE THREATS."

"Ooh, how exciting!" called out a green, shrub-like extraterrestrial in the front row. "How's that for a twist? The robots are going to attack us, too!"

"Help us, Galactic Battle team!" called a blobby creature behind her with a huge smirk, playing along. "We're in terrible danger."

"You don't know the half of it!" John said under his breath. "Um, Zepp, any time you want to step in – that's fine with me!"

"I am not authorized to override the Defendroids, John," Zepp answered.

The Defendroids had begun moving purposefully now, heading for the edge of the stage. Within moments, they would be wading through the defenceless families in the audience. If Zepp wasn't going to put a stop to the battle, John had to do something – and fast!

He thought back to the ancient warfare simulations he'd played on his computer back at home. How had the Spartans beaten back the Persians? How had the Roman Empire conquered half the world? *Formation, that's the key!*

The Defendroids had begun swinging their weapon arms threateningly. They purposefully took one step forward and then another, as if they had all the time in the world. Their eyes glowed as fiercely as hot coals.

Some parents had begun stamping and chanting, "Fight! Fight! Fight!" Not one of them showed any sign of knowing the danger they were in.

In his mind's eye, John saw the Battle of Hastings as his old school's history teacher had explained it – the swordsmen in front, the spearmen at the flanks, and the archers at the rear.

Time for a bit of old-fashioned Earth tactics! John thought.

"We need to go into defensive formation," he said urgently. "Kaal, Monix, you guys in front! Keep the robots at bay!"

The two LaserPro wielders bravely ran to stop the

Defendroids in their tracks, holding up their weapons like an energized barrier. *Good, swordsmen in position*, John assured himself.

"Kritta and Tarope, you take the sides! Don't let anything circle round past us!"

"Right!" Tarope yelled. They ran to join Kaal and Monix.

Spearmen at the flanks, John thought. *And now for the archers.*

"Dyfi, get up on my shoulders! We'll fire over Kaal and Monix's heads, OK?"

Dyfi scrambled up John's back and straddled his shoulders. "Ready to rumble, leader!" she said firmly.

John ran and stood behind Kaal and Monix. At the sides, Kritta and Tarope had their SonicArrows ready. The formation was complete.

"Don't let any of them through," John said. "Steady!"

Just then, the Defendroids broke into a run. Four came pounding straight towards Kaal and Monix. John saw that Kaal's LaserPro was trembling in his grasp.

The other two robots – Slicer and Dicer – broke away from the group and headed around the sides of the Galactic Battle formation, making straight for the front row of the audience.

Screams rang out – but they were screams of delight.

"They're coming to get us!" someone howled.

But Kritta and Tarope were in the right place to stop them. Kritta slammed a SonicArrow into Slicer's knee, sending the Defendroid crashing down. On the other side, Tarope's shot struck the already battered Dicer right on the front of its head, where Dyfi's shots had previously melted it. The SonicArrow pierced the metal and went in deep.

Dicer crackled all over with electricity, gave a low moan like a dinosaur falling into a tar pit, and crashed down, defeated.

Tarope gave a whoop of victory. "And Dicer is *toast*!"

"Don't celebrate yet," John warned. "Still five more left!"

Kaal and Monix stood their ground, their LaserPros weaving a barrier of bright light. The Defendroids advanced, fell back, and advanced again. They seemed to sense that coming too close to the bright, slashing energy swords could be fatal.

But that made them easy targets for the Hot Shots. John loosed off round after round, peppering the Defendroids with white-hot spots the size of saucers. Their metal armour hissed and fizzled where the pellets struck.

Dyfi clung on tight to his shoulders – *ouch!* – and let loose a flurry of shots of her own.

"We're not doing enough damage!" she yelled.

"Aim for their control panels!" John yelled back. "And change to rapid fire!"

"Now you're talking," Dyfi said. She altered the setting on her Hot Shot, and she and John concentrated their fire on Steel Storm, who was looming above Kaal and Monix.

John's Hot Shot bucked in his hand as the relentless volley of superheated missiles hammered the Defendroid. Steel Storm's chest grew first cherry red, then searing orange under the onslaught.

Roaring wildly, and waving its fist, the robot staggered backward. The stench of burning metal was strong in the air.

Then, without warning, Steel Storm lunged forward

and struck. Its mighty wrecking-ball fist slammed into the stage with the force of a missile. Painful shocks shot up John's legs as the electric blast detonated, knocking him off his feet. The Galactic Battle team was flung like skittles, tumbling across the stage in different directions. With a yell, Dyfi went flying off his shoulders.

"TARGETS NEUTRALIZED," rumbled Steel Storm.

John rolled over and over, wincing in pain, and then got up on one knee.

Quickly, he took stock of the situation. The team was scattered, but nobody looked badly hurt. Of the Defendroids, Dicer was out of action, Slicer was still trying to stand up with Kritta's SonicArrow embedded in its knee, and the other four were swivelling their arms and legs around, heading away from the team and towards the crowd.

They think we're dealt with and no longer dangerous, so they're turning to the audience again! The only way to save the families is to show these robots we're still a threat ...

John leaped to his feet. "Monix, Kaal, finish Slicer off!" he yelled. "Everyone else, open fire on the droids. We've got to get their attention."

With Kaal close behind, Monix zoomed across the stage to where Slicer was floundering. As she drew close, the Defendroid suddenly swiped at her with its huge blade arm, drawing *oohs* and *aahs* from the crowd.

She blocked the blow with milliseconds to spare, and hissing sparks flew from her LaserPro, as it dragged down the edge of the blade.

The droid is running a decoy routine. It isn't that badly hurt – it just wanted to get her close!

"Oh no, you don't," Kaal said, as Slicer drew back its arm for another blow.

With one stroke, Kaal slashed through its arm at the wrist, and the great blade fell with a clatter and clang. Kaal's next stroke sheared through Slicer's neck.

The Defendroid's head fell from its body and hit the ground with a sound like thunder. Sparks jetted from the stump. The head rolled to the edge of the stage, fell off, rolled a little way further, and came to a stop in front of the stunned audience ...

Who promptly went berserk.

Why isn't Lorem doing anything to help? John

wondered. It didn't take an ability to see into the future to realize that something was going seriously wrong!

Meanwhile, Tarope and Kritta pelted the remaining Defendroids with SonicArrows, while John and Dyfi bombarded them with heat pellets.

"Come on!" John yelled. "We're the threat here! Turn around and face us!"

And slowly, the Defendroids did just that. Steel Storm's head craned around, focusing at John, seemingly calculating what level of danger he represented.

"They're going to charge us again!" Kritta warned.

"Formation!" John yelled.

Kaal and Monix rejoined the group, panting from exertion, and took up their position in the vanguard.

Kaal glanced back at John, his face spattered with oil. "I'm going to get Mordant for this," he said.

"You and me both," John said, reloading his Hot Shot and realizing that Kritta was right: the Defendroids were mustering for another charge.

"And as for G-Vez, he can start a new life as our dormitory waste bin!" John said. "Once I've ripped his circuits out, that is!" John was furious, but he made himself focus on the task at hand. "Now hold steady, everyone – they're coming!"

Now the Defendroids had assumed a formation of their own. Lasher was in front of the robot charge. Basher and Crusher had moved to either side, and Steel Storm looked on from the rear.

We can't stay on the defensive for ever, John thought. *They'll just keep coming!*

He quickly unleashed a rapid-fire stream of heat pellets at Lasher, trying to hit the crucial control panel. The Defendroid staggered, but it didn't slow down. Then, all at once, it brought its arm around in a wide arc, aiming for the team's feet.

Kaal leaped into the air, beating his wings, with Monix close behind. The arm whizzed past. Tarope bounded out of the way. But Dyfi, Kritta, and John were knocked onto the floor.

The audience gasped.

John had almost fallen off the edge of the stage.

Steel Storm was moving now, thundering towards him. "ENEMY LEADER IDENTIFIED," it buzzed. "DESTROY. DESTROY."

John had one chance. With forced calm, he brought his Hot Shot up and aimed between Steel Storm's red eyes. He pulled the trigger.

Click.

Out of pellets! He tugged the empty thermal clip out and grabbed at his belt for the next one. But there was nothing there.

I'm out of ammo, he realized, with mounting fear. Time seemed to slow down, and he couldn't see any of his teammates nearby. Steel Storm was bearing down on him, its fist moving like a sledgehammer, a half-ton of lethal electrified metal.

The last thing John Riley would ever see.

CHAPTER 14

In desperation, John flung his empty Hot Shot at the Defendroid's head. There was the tiniest chance he might hit a vital spot and shut it down.

But the Hot Shot bounced off harmlessly. John staggered backward, as the huge metal fist fell towards him.

Instantly, Kaal was there, swooping down from above in a power dive, his LaserPro held out in front of him. He slammed into Steel Storm's back, and the impact drove the energy blade right through the Defendroid's armour and into its inner workings.

Steel Storm bellowed, smoke curling from its

mouth. It grabbed at its back, clutching for Kaal, desperate to crush him. John quickly ducked out of the huge robot's reach and ran to join the rest of the team.

Kaal kicked himself away from Steel Storm and glided in a swooping curve over the heads of the astonished parents, before landing beside John.

"Thanks!" John panted. "I owe you one!"

"What now?" asked Kaal.

The Defendroids were now standing their ground, each one of the remaining four facing out a different direction. They began to stomp their feet on the stage – THOOM, THOOM, THOOM – in a nerve-shattering rhythm.

"They're going to mince whichever one of us goes in first!" Monix said.

I might not be able to fight any more, John thought, *but I can still lead.*

"I'm not falling for that," he told them. "Team, spread out! Encircle them! If any droid moves away from the others, target it!"

The battle-weary team edged around the stage until they had the droids completely surrounded.

The Defendroids continued pounding the stage with their constant reverberating stomps. The audience was clapping along now, still oblivious to the terrible danger.

"Ignore the noise!" John yelled. "The droids are trying to scare you! Don't let them!"

Suddenly, Crusher broke ranks, singling out Kritta and charging at her with a raised arm and bellowing like a runaway train.

"All on Crusher!" John yelled. "NOW!"

Kritta stood bravely in the robot's path, gripping her SonicArrow. Kaal and Monix ran in to help, slashing at Crusher's legs. Kritta threw her SonicArrow – and missed. It screamed as it soared over Crusher's head, but hit Basher right in the neck, knocking it to the ground.

As Kritta flung herself out of Crusher's path at the last minute, a blast of scorching heat caught the robot full in the face. It clutched at its eyes.

"VISION IMPAIRED. CANNOT SEE."

"Bullseye!" Dyfi said defiantly, slotting in a fresh clip.

"Monix!" John called. "Finish him!"

Monix darted through the air in a blinding flash, landing one, two, three blows at the flailing robot. Crusher's arms fell off. Followed by its head. The robot torso stood, smouldering like a factory chimney, before it toppled and crashed to the floor.

"And then there were three," John said, with a fierce grin of triumph. "OK, Kaal and Monix, this is going to be dangerous, but I need you to trust me."

"Say the word," said Monix. Kaal just nodded, as if trusting John had become second nature.

"Fly around Lasher's head. Try to lead him towards us. Get as close as you can, but don't attack yet. OK?"

"You got it, boss!" yelled Monix, flying straight towards the remaining Defendroids.

Only Steel Storm kept its distance, as Kaal and Monix began to buzz Lasher, zooming in close and darting away again. Lasher swatted at them with its wrecking ball, but the weapon was too cumbersome to hit a target in flight.

"REQUEST ASSISTANCE," Lasher bellowed.

Come on, Lasher, you stupid great metal lump! John thought. *Take the bait!*

Lasher stepped forward, still swiping at Kaal and

Monix with its wrecking-ball arm. They ducked and weaved – and the ball's chain tangled around Dicer's arm. The two Defendroids tugged hard, trying to pull apart from one another.

"Yes! They're stuck!" John yelled. "Attack now! NOW!"

Kaal swept in from one side, Monix from the other. The LaserPros flashed, two mighty clangs rang out – and two headless Defendroids stood on the stage, smoke pouring from their bodies, hopelessly entangled, unable to fall over.

Only Steel Storm was left. The Defendroid slowly took one step towards John, and then another.

"ENEMY LEADER IS NOT ARMED," it intoned. "MOVING TO INTERCEPT."

"Tarope!" John called, "Get over to Kaal."

"But there'll be nobody to defend you!" Tarope protested.

"That's what I'm counting on," John said with a wink. "Just remember what you and Kaal did in practice, OK?"

Tarope stared at him open-mouthed, before giving him a slow, wide grin. "Got it!"

With John now on his own, Steel Storm tromped towards him, swishing its electric fist like a pendulum ticking down his last moments.

Behind the Defendroid, Tarope skidded to a stop beside Kaal. Both watched John anxiously.

"Come on!" John yelled up at Steel Storm, opening his arms wide. "What are you waiting for? Attack me!"

"STATEMENT IS ILLOGICAL," boomed Steel Storm. "YOU HAVE NO WEAPON. YOU WILL BE DESTROYED." Blue bolts of electricity sizzled around its steel fist. It pulled back its arm to strike.

"No weapon?" John snarled. "I've got *five*. Kaal! NOW!"

On cue, Kaal flung Tarope into the air, just like he'd done in dress rehearsal. Tarope soared up past the spotlights, and just as he began to fall back down, he threw his SonicArrow with the force of a cannonball. There was something unearthly about the silence as it flew – a silence suddenly broken by a metallic *screech*, as it plunged through the top of Steel Storm's head.

The robot's eyes strobed wildly. It began to spin and totter, totally out of control. Fizzles of lightning spat and crackled across the stage. It immediately went hurly-burlying towards the audience.

"Everyone attack!" John shouted. "Take it down – fast!"

Two SonicArrows whipped into the robot's legs, sending it stumbling. Two LaserPros severed its knee joints. Steel Storm was still thrashing about as it fell, until Dyfi sprang forward and unloaded an entire clip of heat pellets into its chest at point-blank range.

The Defendroid's whole body suddenly froze, all its limbs locked, like a mythical monster unexpectedly turned to stone. The red light in its eyes flickered once, and then died.

John looked around at the smoking remains of the six Defendroids.

We did it, he realized numbly. *We beat them.*

The spotlights suddenly seemed very bright, burning like supernovas in his eyes. There was a strange rushing sound in his ears, too.

But that sound was applause. The audience was in total rapture, cheering and calling out their names.

He felt Monix take his right hand, and Tarope's cool, slimy fingers closed on his left. Kritta, Dyfi, and Kaal joined the chain, and they all took a bow. The applause grew even louder.

Lorem flashed onto the stage. "Would all the teams please join me here?"

Suddenly, the stage was crowded with students, all smiling and staring at John and the team in amazement. He heard voices all around, whispering about the Galactic Battle team, about how they had totally stolen the show. They weren't jealous – they were proud.

"Parents," said Lorem, "please show your appreciation for what I'm sure you will agree has been the most astonishing Space Spectacular in many years!"

The applause was mind-blowing. One parent after another stood up, until the whole auditorium was united in a standing ovation.

CHAPTER 15

It took a long time, but eventually the applause died away. As the members of the Galactic Battle team let go of one another's hands and headed backstage in a daze, Kaal grabbed John's arm.

"I'm so sorry," Kaal said. "I must have done something to make the Defendroids go haywire. I should never have tried to fix them."

"It's my fault," said John. "I told you to do it. And I'd be dead now if it wasn't for you."

A little tunnel led under the Centre, prepared with cold drinks and MorphSeats, ready for the teams to relax on. Immediately, the other students cleared the way, offering the Galactic Battle team their choice of seats.

John threw himself a sofa, laughing with relief, and beginning to shiver with delayed shock. His teammates all piled on with him, Kritta gazing at Kaal in awe.

The big Derrilian was grinning from green ear to green ear.

"Did we really *do* that?" Dyfi asked. "I mean … wow."

"We really did," said Tarope. "I wish the crew back at my old spawning ground could see me now. 'Tarope the wimp' no more!"

"So do you think you've gone out on a high enough note, Monix?" Kritta laughed.

"Oh, you had to bring that up!" Monix said, laughing, too. "You know what? I'm the lucky one."

"*Lucky?*" Kaal said, puzzled. "How?"

"It's my last year here. Nobody's going to expect me to top that performance next year. But you guys, on the other hand … good luck!"

Everyone else laughed, but John could only manage a smile.

"What's wrong, John?" Kritta asked. "We did it! We beat the Defendroids and saved everyone on the ship!"

"I know," John sighed. "I should be happy. I just wish I could have straightened things out with Emmie, that's all."

"So go and talk to her!" Kritta nudged him in the ribs. "She's over there."

John leaped to his feet as he spotted Emmie in the corner of the tunnel, by the drinks machine. "Emmie!"

"We can cope without our fearless leader!" Kritta called. "Don't worry!"

Emmie saw John approaching and immediately seized him in a fierce hug. "Oh, John. I'm so sorry. I should have known, I should have seen! It was Mordant all along!"

John let out a long, relieved sigh. "I thought I'd have to convince you."

"You don't – I know exactly what's been going on. He's been playing mind games with me," Emmie said bitterly. "Everything he's done – coming over all friendly, saying you two had been mean to me – it was all a trick. He wanted to steal my friendship for himself! And I believed him! But I overheard him telling off G-Vez about the Defendroids and I just *knew* he'd been lying."

"But what about your suit?"

"Mordant must have torn it up himself," said Emmie angrily.

John said, "Wait! I saw G-Vez carrying a metal claw in the Junkyard. Mordant must have got him to find it, then used it to rip your suit up so it would look like Kaal had done it!"

Emmie's mouth was an O of astonishment. "That little *creep*! And to think I ran crying to *him*! He was so kind, so supportive, and all the time he was the one doing it!"

"Sounds like the Mordant we all know, huh?"

Emmie wiped her eyes angrily. "Oh, John, I've been so stupid – I should have trusted you from the start!"

At that moment, Mordant came swaggering through the crowd. He went up to Emmie and threw his tentacle around her. "Why are you talking to this jerk?" he asked. "Hey, Riley, you'd better not be bothering her."

With lightning speed, Emmie span around and

slapped him. The noise was as loud as the crack of a whip. Everyone nearby stopped talking and stared.

Mordant touched his cheek, as the black skin reddened. His familiar hateful sneer was suddenly back, as if Emmie had ripped off a mask. "You're an idiot, Tarz," he hissed. "I'm glad I messed with those Defendroids. Too bad they didn't pulverize your precious little friends!"

"At least I *have* friends," Emmie shot back. "And they never turned their back on me. But you'll never know how good that feels."

"Awww," Mordant said. "Cute. You deserve each other."

"Don't ever try to get between me and them again. Got it?"

Mordant glared for a moment, as Kaal came up to complete the group. Then he stormed off, seething, through the crowd. Alone.

"That was awesome," John said.

"He had it coming," Emmie replied with a glare in Mordant's direction. "These last few days have been so horrible. When I think of all the things that have happened … *ugh*."

"Come and sit with us and tell me and Kaal all about it," John suggested. "He's been worried about you, too."

The rest of the Galactic Battle team made room for Emmie on the sofa, and she poured out the story.

"The Neptune nuts were what started it all," she went on. "I found a load grated into my Zorbalene soup."

"You don't like them?" Kaal asked.

"I'm allergic. They make my face swell up. If I'd eaten them, I wouldn't have been able to take part in the Space Spectacular! That's what I meant about ending up in the medical wing. Mordant stopped me just in time – he said he could smell something funny. I was *so* grateful. Now I know the truth." She made a revolted face. "He said he had a hunch who'd done it, so we sneaked into your dorm room …"

"Oh, *now* I get it," John said, remembering the box of Neptune nuts he'd found by his bedside. "Didn't you suspect he'd planted them, though?"

"He'd been with me all day!" Emmie said. "It seemed like it couldn't have been him! And after practice yesterday, I went for my shower and my shampoo bottle was full of jet engine oil." She shuddered at the memory.

"And Mordant led you to our dorm on another 'hunch', didn't he?" Kaal asked angrily. "John, remember the oil smudges on the door panel?"

"Yeah," John said. "He really worked overtime on this one."

"Then there was my suit … He tricked me," Emmie said, and fresh blue tears began to well up. "My two best friends, and I turned on you. I can't believe it. I've been so stupid … Why am I always so STUPID?"

"You are *not* stupid, Emmie," John said firmly. "Mordant played this one like a pro. Anyone would have been taken in."

"He put you all in danger!' she raged. "Sabotaging the Defendroids – everyone's families could have been hurt! We can't let him get away with that!"

"I still don't know how he did it," Kaal confessed. "How could he have found out the codes to put the robots in training mode so he could sabotage them? How did he plant those Neptune nuts and put oil in the shampoo while he was with Emmie?"

John suddenly remembered the tiny metallic shape

he'd seen, hovering up in the shadows in the Belly. It had been there when Master Tronic had given him the code. It hadn't been a bat, it was …

"G-Vez!" he said. "That's how!"

"Of course!" Kaal groaned. "While Mordant was buttering up Emmie, his loyal little droid was out doing his dirty work. G-Vez must have followed us into the Belly and memorized the codes."

"He goes on errands for Mordant all the time," John agreed. "I should have figured it out sooner!"

"Mordant Talliver's got to pay for this," Emmie said in a blood-chilling tone. "He wants to play games? Well, he's going to learn that other people can play them, too. That slap's going to seem like a kiss on the cheek when I'm through with him!"

"You don't need to take revenge on him," John said. "You, Kaal, and I are friends again, and Mordant the saddo is out on his ear. That's the best revenge we could hope for!"

Emmie's scowl immediately dissolved into a smile. "Oh, come here!" She hugged John and Kaal at the same time.

They sat together on the sofa for a while, not saying

a word, and not needing to.

"Attention, all students!" announced Zepp. "The Centre has now been restored to its usual configuration! Any students who wish to meet their parents for an after-show meal may now do so. Have fun!"

The Galactic Battle team sprang up off the sofa. It was time to go their separate ways. Dyfi, Tarope, and Monix all headed up to the Centre, promising to catch up later, while Kaal and Kritta went to speak with their families. Only John and Emmie remained.

"I'd better go," John said.

"No way! Come and meet my folks," she insisted. "They've heard a lot about you!"

Brannicus and Morghaine Tarz, John soon discovered, had heard *everything* about him.

"She never shuts up about you," Brannicus said, his eyes twinkling through blue wrap-around sunglasses. "All these adventures you've had together! Flying shuttles on volcanic worlds, going space-walking with only one of her suit designs to protect you, preventing interplanetary war …"

"Brannicus's colleagues on the Galactic Council

were particularly impressed with that one," said Morghaine. "Tell me, John, do you think Emmie might follow her father into politics?"

"Of course she won't," Brannicus interrupted. "And one galactic diplomat in the family is more than enough, surely!"

"Well, I'm just glad you're here to keep her feet on the ground," sighed Morghaine. She laid a golden hand on John's arm. "Emmie is a bit of a free spirit."

"Yeah," John said. "We like her that way."

Emmie's golden skin blushed, and she gave him a proud grin.

"She takes after her mother," said Brannicus with a wink. "John, I hope you'll join us for a meal?"

"Sure!"

Morghaine waved across the Centre to Kaal's parents. "Vorn! Dulâna! Let's all grab a table together. One big party!"

"If there's one thing my mum knows how to do," Emmie whispered to John, "it's celebrate."

And so, Kaal's parents, Emmie's parents, Kulvi, Emmie, Kaal, and John all ended up crammed into Ska's Café, laughing and gorging themselves on plate after steaming plate of bizarre delicacies. Serve-U-Droids constantly hovered in and out of the room, whisking away empty dishes and bringing in new ones covered in transparent domes.

John created a little island of Earth food at his end of the table, with Zepp's help: sausages, chips, a huge jug of cola with ice, tortillas and dip, ketchup, and for some reason, a little sachet of mango chutney.

"Aha!" cheered Brannicus Tarz, as a Serve-U-Droid brought in a steaming bowl of something purple, along with a little flask of clear liquid. "The Emperor's Delight has arrived!" The bowl was a deep, rich gold, with engraved dragon-like creatures chasing one another around the rim.

"I do confess, I've always wanted to try one of these," Vorn Tartaru said. "A Sillaran delicacy, so I'm told."

"*The* Sillaran delicacy," Morghaine smiled. "No expense spared tonight."

Emmie bounced with excitement. "Can I do the honours? Please?"

Morghaine leaned over to John. "Ever since she was a little girl, it's always been Emmie who ignites the Emperor's Delight. It's a sort of family tradition."

Just like me with the Christmas pudding and brandy, John thought.

Emmie opened the flask and shook in the contents, and a startling column of purple flames roared upward, then died away. "So who gets the lucky first gulp?" she said breathlessly.

Brannicus stood up and passed the bowl to John. "The honour goes to you today, young man."

John could hardly refuse, not after that. He took a small sip. The stuff was like warm fish oil mixed with toenail clippings. He forced himself to smile.

Brannicus nodded, pleased. "Pass the bowl to your right."

John passed it to Kaal, who took a huge, greedy swallow. "Dad, it's *delicious*!"

"Just one gulp, then pass it on!" Brannicus said.

John couldn't help wondering what his own parents would make of all this. Would his dad crack jokes with Kaal's father, while his mother praised Emmie's mum's fashion sense? It was so easy to imagine them here ... and that just made it hurt worse to know that they couldn't be.

Just as he was starting to feel sad again, he felt Emmie's dad put his arm around him.

"You must think of yourself as part of the family, John," he said. "There's always room for you in our house on Sillar, any time you feel like visiting. Maybe you could stay with us for a holiday some time?" He grinned. "Emmie needs someone to go flying with."

"Wow. That would be *really* cool," John said, amazed. "I'd love to!"

Suddenly, in a ball of glowing energy, Lorem appeared beside John. "Pardon me butting in, everyone," he said. "But, John, I wanted to tell you that I have just sent an email to your parents. I thought they deserved to know how hard you have worked on this Space Spectacular, especially in your role as team leader." He smiled slightly. "Naturally, I changed a few details."

"Headmaster," John said, "I have to tell you—"

"About the Defendroids?" Lorem said seriously. "Yes, John, I know the danger you faced was more real than the audience realized."

"You knew? But you didn't stop them! We could

have been hurt, or killed!"

"I saw that you were able to win without my help," Lorem said. "It was your victory. I could not take it away from you. And as for the person responsible ..."

"You know about that, too?"

"What Mordant did was very serious. He didn't just put your team in grave danger – he put the whole audience at risk. He will be spending the rest of term in daily detention, which will give him plenty of time to reflect on matters such as friendship and fair play. The only reason he hasn't been expelled is that he did not intend for you to be harmed – he was only trying to prevent your team from performing. He obviously underestimated your team's determination and spirit." Lorem shook his head. "Young Miss Tarz was right when she said how important it is to have loyal friends. To have no true friends at all ..." Lorem shook his head. "That is a punishment far worse than anything an Examiner could inflict. I would not wish it on anyone."

Suddenly, Zepp's voice broke over the gathering. "Headmaster, I've received an email response from John's parents!"

"If John doesn't mind, please read it out," Lorem said with a smile.

"'Dear headmaster, thank you so much for writing. We are very proud to hear of our son's achievements. It is encouraging to hear how well he is doing at your excellent school. We could not be happier with this news, and we hope you will tell him that.'"

A round of applause rippled around the table. John felt a little embarrassed to be the centre of attention, but also full of pride.

"Thank you, Zepp," Lorem said. "Since John came to Hyperspace High, I have taken something of an interest in Earth literature, and I seem to remember some wise anonymous fellow once said 'leaders are not born, they are made'. I think John has proved that to be true."

Emmie nudged John, beaming. Kaal came around from the other side of the table to join them.

Just then Lorem spoke low so that only John could hear. "You might like to hear another saying I learned from your Earth writers. 'Members of the same family do not always grow up under the same roof.'"

John put his arms around Kaal and Emmie's shoulders – the friends who, he knew, were his family out here in endless space – and grinned. "Or under the same stars."

Here's a sneak preview of the next
Hyperspace High adventure…

SPACE PLAGUE

CHAPTER 1

A fat, black, octopus-like creature with red eyes and a drooling slit of a mouth tapped a tentacle on the desk impatiently. "Well, John Riley, do you know the answer or not?" it slobbered.

John ran a hand through his messy mop of blond hair, his forehead lined in concentration. He leaned forward in his MorphSeat and glanced around the bright classroom, desperately looking for a clue to the answer.

In the seat next to him, a beautiful silver-haired girl from the planet Sillar lifted her shoulders in a shrug. Emmie Tarz didn't know the answer, either.

"Umm ... yes, Doctor Graal," John said eventually. "The soil structure on planet Bezkel is unusual because ... ahhh ..."

"Please stop mumbling and state the answer clearly, so the whole class can hear," interrupted the Gargon teacher.

Blushing, John stammered, "It's unusual b-because there's – you know – alien stuff in it ..."

Doctor Graal glared at him. "That will do, Mister Riley. It is quite obvious that you do *not* know the answer. I shudder to think how you will cope with your exams. If, by some miracle, you pass, I suggest you pay more attention next term." Turning away, she continued, "Who *can* tell me what is unusual about the soil structure on planet Bezkel ... oh, of course. Mordant Talliver."

A few seats along from John, the half-Gargon boy with black hair lowered one of the two long, black tentacles that sprouted from his ribcage. "Every century Bezkel has a ten-year solar eclipse," he answered quickly. "Most plant life dies, producing layers of extremely rich, dark soil. This creates an especially plentiful growing season once the eclipse has passed."

"*Excellent* answer, Mordant," blubbered the teacher. "I'm so glad *someone* has been paying attention."

Mordant shot a sly glance at John. "Learning must be difficult when your brain isn't properly evolved," he whispered, loud enough for John to hear.

Lights flickered across the surface of a small silver sphere that floated at Mordant's shoulder. "How witty you are, young Master Talliver. And how *right*. The Earthling does not deserve to be in the same classroom as you," droned his constant companion, the Serve-U-Droid, G-Vez.

"Yeah, primitive life forms belong in zoos," Mordant sniggered.

Furious, John opened his mouth to retort. A hand gripped his shoulder. Looking round quickly, he saw his friend Kaal shake his head. A native of the planet Derril, Kaal's green skin, sharp fangs, and leathery wings made him look like a demon. In his case, though, looks were deceiving: Kaal was a shy, clever student and a good friend. As John watched, the Derrilian put a finger to his lips.

Blushing an even deeper red, John ground his teeth together. Kaal was right: getting into a fight with Mordant Talliver, especially in Doctor Graal's Galactic Geography class, was asking for trouble. The half-Gargon boy was the teacher's favourite and she was bound to take his side. As Mordant knew well, John would land himself a detention, or worse, if he took the bait. Biting back a retort, John turned back to face Doctor Graal instead, muttering, "Maybe I'd pay more attention in class if *you* ever said anything interesting," under his breath.

Fortunately, the Gargon teacher didn't hear. She had lifted a metal box onto the desk with her tentacles and was busy unfastening the clips that secured its lid. "I have a very exciting sample here," she said. "An important rock formation from the planet Zhaldaria that I found in a storage chamber at the Pan-Galactic Geography Institute during the last school holiday. It hasn't been opened for a very long time but if the label is correct, it should be a perfect example of how a planet's changing weather systems affect its soil structure."

Yay, more soil. Too much excitement, thought

John. As he leaned back in his MorphSeat, it adjusted around his new position. Hearing a sigh from the next desk, he glanced round. Emmie rolled her navy-blue eyes. John winked at her, knowing that his friend was thinking exactly the same thing. Both of them hated Galactic Geography lessons.

At the front of the class, Doctor Graal's eyes lit up as the lid of the box flipped open. "Oh, *yes*," she drooled, "it's a *fine* example. How absolutely wonderful." Two tentacles dipped into the box and pulled out a rock the size of a football. Wobbling forward, she slithered from one desk to the next, showing her exhibit to the students. "Zhaldarian rock is fascinating to study because in ancient times the planet's weather system changed so frequently," she said. "Note the different-coloured bands. Each layer was, at one point in history, the surface of Zhaldaria. By analysing the bands, galactic geologists can tell exactly what happened in the planet's ecosystem over many thousands of years. It is especially rare because Zhaldaria's star – Zaleta – went supernova almost a million years ago, forming the Zaleta Nebula. This small piece of rock is probably all that is left of a once thriving planet."

John leaned forward, trying his best to look interested, as Doctor Graal turned the lump of rock this way and that in front of him. As she moved on, he shrugged.

Yeah, fascinating, he thought.

"What does this band tell us about Zhaldaria's weather?" asked Kaal once Doctor Graal reached his desk, running a finger along a ribbon of black that ran through the centre of the rock.

"Students must *not* touch," snapped the teacher, slapping Kaal's hand away with one of her tentacles. "This sample is extremely old and delicate. To answer your question, the black band dates from the first appearance of Zhaldarian Flu, which wiped out the entire Zhaldarian race before spreading across the universe."

"Ugh," said Kaal, wiping his hand on his silver and red jumpsuit uniform.

Doctor Graal rolled her eyes. "There is no danger. There hasn't been a single case of Zhaldarian Flu in over two hundred years."

A chime sounded, ending the class. Around the

classroom, students chattered while they slipped their portable ThinScreen computers into carry cases.

Gently placing her rock back in its box, Doctor Graal shouted over the noise. "Class dismissed, but do not forget – end-of-term exams begin tomorrow. I expect you all to revise *constantly* until then, especially Emmie Tarz and John Riley. If you fail, you will *not* be returning to Hyperspace High next term."

"I'll send G-Vez to help you both with your packing if you like," Mordant chipped in. "You might as well get started straight away."

Emmie's blue eyes glinted dangerously as she turned on the half-Gargon. "Why don't you do that," she hissed. "It will give me a chance to throw your nasty little droid out of an airlock."

"Oh I say, Master Talliver. Are you going to let her—"

"Do you always have to be such a *jerk*, Mordant?" John cut in, his hands balling into fists.

A grin spread across Mordant Talliver's face.

"Is there a problem, Mordant?" Doctor Graal called over.

"John just called me a—"

"There's no problem, Doctor Graal," Kaal interrupted with a forced laugh. "We're just joking around." Taking John's shoulder with one enormous hand and Emmie's with the other, he pushed them both through the door and into the corridor outside. "John and Emmie were just saying they're on their way to revise right now," he bellowed over his shoulder, drowning out Mordant's indignant protests as he steered his friends through the crowd of students leaving the classroom.

Once they'd bumped and jostled their way out of Doctor Graal's earshot, the Derrilian crossed his arms and sighed. "That wasn't very sensible," he said. "You know Mordant's trying to get you into trouble before exams."

"I know," said John. "I can't help it. He's such a—"

"Spiteful, smug, arrogant waste of atoms," Emmie finished for him, hooking long silvery hair behind one of her pointed ears and scowling. "What's his problem anyway? Does he wake up every morning and think 'I'm going to be a vile, obnoxious bully today'?"

Kaal passed a hand across his face – the Derrilian equivalent of a shrug, John had learned – then patted

Emmie on the shoulder. "Gargons," he said, "you know what they're like. Can't you just ignore him?"

"Huh," Emmie snorted. "I haven't forgotten what he did during the Space Spectacular. He tried to wreck my friendship with you guys."

"It would be great if we *could* ignore him," said John, "but he's really good at winding us up. He *knows* Emmie and I are worried about failing the exams, and with me only being here by accident ..."

Read
SPACE PLAGUE
to find out what happens next!

For more exciting books from brilliant
authors, follow the fox!
www.curious-fox.com